# A Cinderella for His Lordship

A Clean Regency Romance Novel

Martha Barwood

Copyright © 2022 by Martha Barwood
All Rights Reserved.
This book may not be reproduced or transmitted in any form without the written permission of the publisher. In no way is it legal to reproduce, duplicate, or transmit any part of this document in either electronic means or in printed format. Recording of this publication is strictly prohibited and any storage of this document is not allowed unless with written permission from the publisher.

# Table of Contents

# Prologue

Catriona could hardly squeeze her hands shut by the time she had finished in the kitchen. The blisters threatened to pop each time she did so. Thinking better of it, she decided to head up to her room. The kitchen was cleaned, anyway. No one could bother her for more work now.

As she walked to her room, she became aware of a pounding in her head—like someone taking dishes and breaking them against her forehead with great force. A migraine. Great. That would make her work tomorrow even harder than it already would be. Why had she not been adopted by a nice family when she was younger, like many of the others?

That might have made her life easier, but for now, she had to comply with the ridiculous demands the orphanage made of her. If they wanted her to clean the entire kitchen, practically alone, then she couldn't really argue. Not if she didn't want to get tossed into the streets and left to survive all on her own . . . which she knew would not end well. She'd be able to get a position as a maid, of course, but that would only get her so far.

While a proper position might have paid her, she had a feeling that the weariness she felt now would never end if she took that work up outside the orphanage too.

Upon arriving at her room, Catriona found Alice sitting on the other bed. A soft smile pulled at Catriona's lips. At least she had her good friend to suffer with her through all of this.

"Catriona . . . you look *knocked up* . . ." Alice pursed her lips and frowned, showing more concern than Catriona had ever seen in one so young.

"What else can I do?"

She sighed as she sat down on her bed, taking her shoes off. Someone had broken a few plates earlier that morning, and she had spent the entire day with her boots on. The pain became more noticeable as her stockings slid around the blisters that had formed from wearing shoes that were both falling apart and at least one size too small.

"You could perhaps not work yourself to the bone. Those blisters look painful . . ." Alice winced, looking at them.

"Well . . . if we don't comply, they'll cast us onto the street, you know," Catriona replied bitterly. "Is it possible to feel any less worthy of a family based on the way they treat us here?"

"I don't know."

Alice lay back on her bed.

"But have you ever wondered what life would be like if we had grown up in a wealthy family, Catriona? Having maids, and lady's maids, and attending all the social events of the year?" She turned to face Catriona. "Having our pick of the men of the town, knowing there was little anyone else could say about it?"

"Money isn't everything, Alice."

"Isn't it, Catriona? When you have nothing, it feels like it . . . what do you think is more valuable than money?"

Alice's brows furrowed deeply as she thought hard about what could be more valuable than money.

"I think what matters most is love. It's what keeps families together when there is nothing left in the bank," she said eventually. "A family who can weather even the worst financial troubles together is the kind of family I want to live in. As it is, we've already weathered the worst life has to throw us. How much worse can it get?"

"Don't say things like that, Catriona!"

Alice pushed herself up, leaning on her elbows and turning to face her friend with such a serious face, Catriona wondered what she had said that was so wrong.

"What do you think is going to happen? We've already lost our families . . . or they didn't want us," Catriona scoffed. "We have no recourse to have a good life here. Not if we haven't already been adopted, after all."

"There's always hope of being adopted. Always. You never know when some baron or some such upper-class person will need someone to pass their wealth off to in old age," Alice warned. "I'm serious!"

"You're being superstitious again, Alice." Catriona shook her head. "I'm exhausted. This isn't a conversation to be having right now. They'll be angry with us if we're up much longer."

"But it's the only time we have to talk, now," Alice whined quietly. "What if you came and sat on my bed, or I sat on yours, and we whispered?"

Catriona smiled, but she had no wish to continue the conversation. The pounding in her head had been growing worse as they talked, and she wanted nothing more than to blow their candles out and try to get some rest.

"I'm too exhausted to talk about anything, Alice. Though, I admit, I don't get many nights when I'm not anymore," she said with a regretful smile. "And I didn't get much to eat today. My body needs rest."

Alice huffed quietly but relented. There was really nothing more to say other than goodnight.

As Catriona blew her candle out, she watched the darkness encroach a little further into the room. The only thing that kept the room from being pitch black at night was the window they were lucky enough to have. It faced the moon most nights in the spring, and she had always found the moon to be a comforting sight. The image would give her some solace during the next day's toil.

In a world of dreary constants, the moonlight and the soft, silvery gleam it threw over London at night made her feel as if she was a princess, if only for a moment.

That thought drifted off into sleep with her, and Catriona dreamed of a palace, large and airy, with many grand halls. There, no one could tell her what to do or how to act. Or what to clean. When to go to bed. It was a place of refuge, of happiness. Alice was there, of course, as was the man she'd always dreamt she'd marry. A man who cared for her personality and not that she had grown up in an orphanage and lacked the more refined sensibilities of the upper classes.

All too soon, the early light of the rising sun wakened Catriona. She sighed and rubbed her eyes. She'd have to get down to the kitchen immediately, as breakfast was to be served soon. It was the one meal during the day when there was a little more leniency about a few minutes lateness because it was so early and everyone was tired.

Alice was still fast asleep in the other bed, which Catriona did her best to respect. After a few years of living at the orphanage, she knew all the creakiest spots on their chamber floor and how to avoid them.

Breakfast didn't demand any special preparations, but even those took some skillful maneuvering to keep her hands and feet from starting to hurt as badly as they had the night before. Thankfully, dish duty seemed to help. She could balance the plates and other flat surfaces on the palm of her hands and press with the areas that didn't have as many blisters as the rest.

It was shortly after she had finished preparing breakfast and started on luncheon that Mrs. Easton came into the room.

"May I see you in my office, Catriona?"

The unexpected summons made her nervous. It had been a while since Mrs. Easton had wanted to see her specifically, and in her office, too. That was never a good sign when one was as old as Catriona. It meant one of two things.

Either Catriona was being adopted by an older couple looking to have someone to help ease things in their older age, or she was being kicked out of the orphanage on the pretext of some imaginary slight Mrs. Easton had dreamed up because she wanted Catriona's bed for a younger child who was more likely to get adopted.

Her stomach tightened upon entering the office and finding a stern man sitting at the desk. He wore a suit, entirely black, with the exception of a golden pocket watch trailed across his vest. The gentleman stood upon seeing her and gave a soft bow at the waist.

"As you requested, sir, Miss Fraiser."

"What a pleasure it is to meet you. I am Mr. Dilworth," the man said.

Catriona couldn't entirely read what was going on, but it was quite clear that Mrs. Easton deferred to Mr. Dilworth in this matter of business—whatever it was.

"Your presence is urgently required at Beaumore Manor in Mayfair, Miss Fraiser," Mr. Dilworth continued, "There is to be a reading of a particular will there tomorrow, and it is imperative that you attend in person."

"Mayfair? But that's so far away, and I have no means of travel, Mr. Dilworth," Catriona said.

"Worry about none of that. I've made all the necessary travel arrangements for the morning as well as hired a lady called Mrs. Burton to be a chaperone tomorrow. You'll be staying the night in a hotel tonight." Mr. Dilworth then turned to Mrs. Easton. "She will no longer need her place here."

"You've heard Mr. Dilworth, Catriona. Go and pack what you wish now and return here immediately afterward."

Catriona only nodded her head and quietly excused herself. Mr. Dilworth and Mrs. Easton said nothing as she left, and she could only assume they were waiting until she was entirely out of earshot before saying anything more about whatever was going on. Clearly, they didn't want her to hear it.

When she returned to her room, Alice was up and preparing to scrub the floors elsewhere in the orphanage. Catriona could tell it by the large apron Alice had wrapped around her slight form.

"I don't usually see you back up here before I go to scrub the floors . . ." Alice said, frowning. "What's going on?"

"I-I . . . I have no idea." Catriona sat down on the bed.

"Well, something has happened to put you in such a daze," Alice said, sitting down beside her friend and looking at her closely.

"Someone has called for me. A Mr. Dilworth. I've just spoken to him; he's with Mrs. Easton in her office. She sent me back up here. It seems I'm to go to Beaumore Manor tomorrow . . . Beaumore Manor, Alice!" She turned to face her friend, eyes wide. "What can it mean? Do you remember last night? You said something about wondering what it would have been like to grow up with a wealthy family . . . Is it possible . . . that I'm about to find out?"

Alice shrugged.

"Perhaps. Did they tell you *why* you've been asked to go to Beaumore Manor?"

"Yes, a will reading, apparently. And my presence, Mr. Dilworth says, is required for it," Catriona explained, her forehead wrinkling. "But why? And why me?"

"Well, the only way to find out is to go to the will reading, I suppose. I hope its good news for you." Alice stood up wearily. "I'd better get to work. We can catch up tonight,"

"No. I . . . I mean, I shan't see you tonight. Mr. Dilworth has arranged for me to stay in a hotel tonight before leaving for the manor tomorrow." Catriona looked at her friend again as Alice reached the door and turned back in surprise. "I'll write to you if I'm not coming back. I hope I will be. But they've asked me to pack my belongings," she explained, adding, "and I don't wish to leave you here."

Alice smiled crookedly. "Catriona, if anyone can survive here, it's me," she said, though her eyes shone a little, hinting at held-back tears. "You deserve a good change in fortune. Now, don't worry about me. I must get to scrubbing those floors, unfortunately, but I hope to hear more from you soon. You know where I am, so, yes, write to me. And if you are to have a new address, you can send it to me—so I can let you know if anything *amazing* happens to me." With a quick wink and a smile, she was gone, closing the door behind her.

Catriona nodded at the closing door, suddenly alone with her thoughts, and her few belongings.

She dragged the small travel trunk she owned out from underneath the bed. It was required of the orphanage to provide everyone with at least one travel trunk for their clothing and such, in case they were ever adopted. Since Catriona had not been adopted as a child, she still had the same small-sized trunk.

It didn't really matter, she soon realized. She only had a couple of outfits she really wanted to take. Then there was her work clothing, which she didn't know if she would need at the manor. The feeling of not knowing what awaited her at the manor made her feel more than simply apprehensive.

It *worried* her. Whatever happened at the manor on the morrow, something had already transpired that required her presence there. As much as she wanted to believe it was because she was going to be meeting her real family after all these years, she couldn't entirely shake off her feelings of uncertainty. It was quite overwhelming.

It didn't help that her packing took mere minutes, leaving her little time to think before she presented herself to Mr. Dilworth once more and was whisked away by him to spend the night at a hotel.

## Chapter One

Hamish had arrived in London two days earlier, but he had not yet seen his parents. However, he had received an invitation to dine with them at Ashington Manor, with the Earl of Ashington and his family. It was their preferred residence during London's social season in London. The arrangement made him wonder what was afoot, since his father seldom did anything without an ulterior motive that would benefit him.

Upon his arrival at Ashington Manor, Henry, the butler, greeted Hamish with a respectful bow and a warm smile.

"Welcome, sir, and thank you for coming. Please, come this way." Henry motioned him inside. "Everyone is waiting in the drawing room for you."

"Thank you, Henry."

Henry walked him to the drawing room, where the door stood open and faint conversation could be heard inside. Hamish was pleased to enter and immediately spot his mother sitting upon one of the small couches. Seeing him, she rose from her seat and walked over to embrace her son heartily.

"It's such a pleasure to have you home again, Hamish," she said with a warmth only his mother could give him. "How was your trip?"

"It was long, but worth it, Mother," Hamish said. "I am quite glad you were able to find time to see me so soon after arriving home."

"Of course, we wanted to see you as soon as you arrived home," his father said, typically not even bothering with a greeting. "Trips are all very well, but there's work to be done here. Now, pay attention, Son. As you will have realized, we are joining the Earl of Ashington and his family for dinner. Now the Season is upon us, the earl will want to take advantage of being in Town and hear all about how business is going in the Far East. That's where you come in—you'll have the most recent knowledge of anyone at the table, having just arrived from there."

"Of course, Father," Hamish replied, sighing inwardly.

"Furthermore, it would be a wise business move if you were to marry the earl's eldest daughter—her name's Lady Josette Ashington." His father paused to give him a stern look, as if to nip any protest in the bud. "She'll do quite well in a marriage with you, I'm sure, and the union will bring us many benefits in expanding our business interests, not to mention a tidy dowry."

"I shall consider it, Father," Hamish said.

But his voice felt strained, and he wondered if his father could tell how unhappy he was to be back in the same situation he had previously escaped from by going abroad. Half the reason he had gone to the Far East to look study business from that side of the trading system was because his father had a particular tick that annoyed Hamish to no end: No matter what Hamish thought was best for his own life, his father would attempt to overrule it and force his son to do whatever he thought best.

This evening's dinner and proposed marriage was typical of his father. Hamish seethed silently. *I've only been in London for a few days, and the old man is already attempting to pull strings to improve the family's business prospects by using me as his pawn!* Though his mother was standing right next to him—he didn't want to upset her—he wondered if it would be worth just walking out and refusing to attend the dinner with the Ashington family.

Never mind that they were his father's longest-standing trading partners, Hamish now found a fresh reason for him to dislike them— Lady Josette Ashington.

He had no time for acting on his thoughts, for dinner was soon announced. The Countess of Ashington, Hamish saw as they entered the dining room, had managed the seating arrangements so that he had no choice but to sit beside Josette. This led Hamish to wonder if his father had already proposed the idea of a marriage of convenience to the earl before Hamish had even set foot back in London.

"How was the Far East, Hamish?"

Josette asked, clearly under orders to entertain him with her conversation. However, aside from allowing him to answer that single question, which he did only briefly, he soon found that most of their conversation thereafter centered on what Josette had been doing while he had been abroad. Apparently, she had become more proficient on the pianoforte, and she had heard that the weather was going to be glorious for the next few weeks.

Hamish could only give a quiet sigh of relief once he got into his carriage at the end of the night. In the Far East, he had not needed to put on air and graces for the sake of business. It had been business and business only in their meeting rooms. Plus, making friends with people not of British descent was something he'd found easier there compared to here in London, within the *ton*, with people like the Ashmore family.

***

It was only the next morning when Hamish had the chance to do what he had wanted to do since arriving back in London. He put on a simple, black three-piece suit, his silver pocket watch displayed on a chain. In his top hat, cane in hand, he set out to board the carriage.

"And where would you like to go today, sir? Beaumore Manor, is it?" The coachman looked at Hamish as if nothing had changed in the time he had been away.

Hamish appreciated the lack of fuss.

"Yes, please. Beaumore Manor, as quickly as you can."

The coachman doffed his hat and waited for Hamish to settle into the carriage before geeing up the horses and setting off. Inside, Hamish found himself in an excited mood; he could hardly believe his long-term plan was finally taking shape. During Hamish's time in the Far East, Anthony Beaumont of Beaumore Manor had kept in touch with him. With Anthony being one of his childhood friends, Hamish had appreciated it.

Now Hamish was back in town, he wanted to see through his plan to go into business with Anthony. The notion felt to him miles better than having to enter a marriage of convenience simply to please his father. And especially not with one of the Ashmore sisters.

Dinner last night had only reinforced his conviction. But he shook the thought away as he arrived at the Beaumore Manor. He was sure Anthony would be as pleased to see him as he was to see his old friend. Their reunion was something they had discussed in their last letter. Anthony had stressed that Hamish should come to see him at the manor at the earliest opportunity.

It wasn't many minutes before Hamish was welcomed inside, and the two friends were sitting opposite one another in Anthony's study.

"It is truly a great blessing to see you again, Hamish," Anthony said with a wide smile. "I will have to hear all the stories you haven't yet told me in your letters from the Far East."

"And, again, I must offer my condolences on the loss of your uncle," Hamish said. "They only go so far in letters. So, Viscount Beaumore . . . what does it feel like to have others address you by your new title when you go out in public?"

"It's been . . . well, it was difficult at the start, I kept forgetting. But it's been six months now." Anthony sighed. "I almost can't believe it's been six months since my father passed away . . . but he hung on as long as he could."

"I'm sorry. It must be painful to talk about. Well, let us be more cheerful and arrange to catch up at the club later tonight or perhaps one evening this week," Hamish suggested, and Anthony nodded, looking relieved not to have to dwell on the loss of his father.

Hamish continued by saying, "One of the reasons for my visit today, apart from seeing you, old friend, is that I wondered if you've had a chance to consider my business proposal any further. I know the timing of my letter was very ill, but there is nothing I could have done to prevent that."

Anthony nodded. "I have given thought to it, and I'm more than happy to go into business with you. Knowing you, and your work, I think it would benefit both of us. And you would have an area of business of your own which would not require you to dazzle someone else before getting the deal you want. You've dazzled me enough with your commitment to staying in the Far East for so long," Anthony said.

Breaking off, he suddenly glanced at his pocket watch, then at a letter laying in front of him on his desk before looking back at Hamish.

"Oh . . . I didn't realize how time had flown," he said regretfully. "I'm sorry, Hamish, but I have to cut this meeting short. I'd love to meet up again soon to further discuss things, though."

"May I ask why? Is that letter urgent?" Hamish asked, peering at it.

"Yes. I've just received urgent word from my uncle's solicitor, Dilworth," Anthony explained, gesturing to the letter. "He says he must meet with me without delay, this morning. In fact, I think he's likely already arrived."

"Oh, well . . . any idea what the meeting is about?"

Anthony shrugged as he stood up.

"It's probably just something more to do with my uncle's will. Mr. Dilworth has been rather . . . secretive about it, and I've not been able to find out why. Thought it best just to wait it out," Anthony said. "Please, come by tomorrow afternoon. I propose a round of fencing and a few drinks afterward. I wish to hear more stories of the Far East."

"And we might discuss the matter of our business too, please. I am incredibly excited at the thought of it, Anthony," Hamish said with a smile.

"Not if we are to catch up," Anthony said, shaking his head. "But we can fix time for a proper business meeting after that. I promise. If I don't do it soon enough for your liking, you're more than welcome to schedule something and force me to sit down. I'm still adjusting to things after my father's death, you see. And it sounds as if the whole family was ready for this meeting, except me. I wonder if they all knew about it."

"Well, if not, they might be in for just as much of a shock as you could be."

"Perhaps so." Anthony shrugged, then cocked an ear. "Do I hear a carriage drawing up to the manor?"

He walked to the window to look out. Hamish did not follow; he was on his feet, about to leave. As disappointing as it was to learn that his friend did not have time to properly discuss their proposed venture that day, it was not Anthony's fault. If the solicitor thought it necessary to spring this meeting on his friend at the last minute, Hamish guessed there was probably something in the will he had not been able to reveal until all the proper conditions were met.

"I was right," Anthony said from the window. "There's a carriage out there, and it's not yours. I'll send word to the stables when we head downstairs."

"Thank you, Anthony," Hamish said. "I hope this meeting brings you good tidings. You deserve it after all that has happened over the last six months."

"I appreciate that, Hamish. You have no idea how much I wanted to run away to the Far East and speak to you personally when I heard Father was so drastically ill. I'm only sorry you could not be here for the funeral."

"I'm sorry too, but it was simply not possible. It's a very long and often arduous journey from the Far East, you know," Hamish said.

Anthony nodded.

As they left the study and went down the hall, Anthony paused to instruct a footman to have Hamish's carriage brought round to the front of the house.

"Do you have any idea what's in your father's will, anyway?" Hamish asked as they came to the stairs and started downwards.

"None." Anthony said, shaking his head. "All I know is that shortly after he fell ill, he became very worried he wouldn't survive longer than a month, so he had the will rewritten. Apparently, Mr.

Dilworth was the only one allowed into the room. Not even my mother was there when the will was rewritten."

Hamish pursed his lips. "How odd," he said as they reached the bottom of the stairs and stood in the main hall.

"Well, I suppose there's nothing to do now but to hear what Mr. Dilworth has to say," Anthony said, his expression serious even as he smiled at Hamish.

"And learn whatever secrets your father has been hiding," Hamish suggested, wiggling his eyebrows as he returned the smile. "I hope all goes well, my friend. You can count on me being here tomorrow for fencing and drinks."

"Good. I can fill you in then," Anthony said with a slight laugh. "I have a feeling it's going to be an odd sort of day." He looked over at the doors Hamish knew led into the drawing room. Voices could be heard faintly from inside. "From the sounds of it, everyone else is already gathered in the drawing room," he added, turning back to Hamish.

"Don't worry, I can see myself out. You go and join your family, and I'll be around if you need a listening ear for any woes or worries," Hamish told his friend with a smile.

The two men shook hands warmly, and Hamish sensed the tension Anthony must be feeling at what might transpire at this meeting when his father's new will was finally read. Would it explain why it had taken so long for it to happen, and would the outcome it benefit Anthony? He hoped it would not be bad news, for his friend's sake.

These thoughts occupied him as he settled once more in his carriage. But they were soon overtaken as he realized his short meeting with Anthony left him with time on his hands. He'd supposed their reunion would take up more time, hoping it would rid him of some of the lingering annoyance he still felt about the previous evening's dinner. He frowned as he thought of how there had been something about sitting so close to Lady Josette Ashmore that had rubbed him up the wrong way.

# Chapter Two

Catriona rose from her luxurious bed in the hotel the next morning still feeling uncertain about what the day held for her. The hotel offered her comfort far more lavish than any conditions she had ever experienced in her life. A lady of her lowly means walking into a posh hotel had earned her quite a few stares from staff and guests the previous evening, even when accompanied by Mrs. Burton, who had the room next door to Catriona.

The sweet-smelling, downy, soft bed had provided her with some of the best sleep ever, with as many thick blankets as she wanted, and plump pillows to sink into. It had been an entirely welcome change from the orphanage's worn-out beds, with their hard metal frames and threadbare blankets that were strictly rationed by the staff.

As she looked into the clear looking glass, she pulled her hair into a tight chignon and took a good look at her face. Her light blonde hair fell in loose wisps around her face, much to her annoyance. But the chignon seemed appropriate if she was to be in polite company that day. Her large, azure blue eyes stared back at her, and she noted with some satisfaction that they looked unusually bright due to the wonderful night's rest she'd had. *Whatever the day brings, I shall not be doing any cleaning at the orphanage today.*

Slender in frame and of average height, Catriona could not fathom what it was about her that made Mr. Dilworth think she was worth a trip to Beaumore Manor. She didn't have a family, that she was well aware of, and she had nothing more to offer than her services as a well-trained maid to this particular family.

*What a shame I have nothing to wear but this old grey dress, worn out from many days of cleaning, and these worn-out shoes.*

But there is nothing to be done about it, she told herself, taking in a deep breath to steel herself for the day ahead. *It won't be long now before I'm in the carriage on the way to Beaumore Manor.*

Indeed, it wasn't long at all. Mrs. Burton made quick work of making sure that Catriona was ready for the day before escorting her out to the waiting carriage. To her, the vehicle seemed just as lavish inside as the hotel, and it made Catriona feel unsettled.

"How long is the drive to Beaumore Manor, Mrs. Burton?" Catriona asked, attempting to make conversation with the chaperone and find out anything she knew.

It got her nowhere. Mrs. Burton told her only that the journey would be two hours or so before clamming up. Her silence did nothing to help ease Catriona's nerves about what to expect. *Why am I being kept in the dark?*

Her nerves heightened when the carriage finally came to a halt outside a large, grand house, which she assumed was their final destination, Beaumore Manor. As the carriage door opened, Catriona gulped hard and her heart raced. She was in such a nervous state, she almost missed the helping hand offered by a footman to help her out of the carriage.

She took the hand and descended to the ground. Soon, in a daze, she found herself being escorted to the entrance of the manor, with Mrs. Burton close behind her. The stone steps felt warm beneath her feet, reminding her of just how threadbare the soles of her shoes were.

Halfway up the steps to the entrance, the sight of a striking gentleman ahead caught her eye. He was tall, and from what she could see of his frame beneath his suit, muscular and well-built, with broad shoulders. He was clean-shaven, and she thought him quite handsome without any of the whiskers or other facial hair some men cultivated.

Then, Catriona realized she seemed to have caught the gentleman's eye too. Blushing before she looked away, she noticed they were such a striking pale blue, and a vision of a summer sky sprang to her mind, almost making her forget where she was.

She bowed her head and attempted to walk past the man without drawing further attention to herself. But before she went any further, she suddenly tripped on the uneven old steps and lost her footing.

As she fell, the gentleman simply reached over, took her arm firmly, and set her upright before she could hurt her face on the stone steps. Only when she seemed steady did he release her arm.

"Are you all right, Miss?" he asked in a deep voice that thrilled her, even in her shaken and mortified state.

Catriona stared at him, managing only a nod of thanks, struck suddenly dumb in the face of his kindness.

He opened his mouth as if about to say more, but someone cleared their throat pointedly, so he shut it again, looking behind Catriona. She didn't have to see her chaperone to realize Mrs. Burton was standing there.

"Have a good day, Miss, Madam," he said hurriedly, tipping his hat to them both before continuing on his way down the steps. Catriona had no choice but to continue into the house, unsure of what had made her trip. She felt somewhat irked that Mrs. Burton hadn't allowed the man to introduce himself to her before leaving.

Then again, she didn't know what kind of society she was getting herself into there at the manor. Surely, it was unusual for someone of his stature to be kind to someone like her. And that only made her wonder again why Mr. Dilworth had insisted she come to Beaumore Manor that day.

An elderly man met her and Mrs. Burton at the door.

"Ah, you must be Miss Fraiser and Mrs. Burton. Mr. Dilworth warned us to expect you today. I am Mr. Leonard, the butler here." He gave a soft bow to both Catriona and Mrs. Burton. "Miss Fraiser, if you'd please follow me. You're needed in the drawing room upstairs."

"I shall wait down here, if you do not mind, sir," Mrs. Burton said.

Leonard nodded and arranged for the chaperone to be seated in a small parlor off the hall. He then escorted Catriona up the impressive staircase. The downstairs of the manor was beautiful, from what she could see of it, but the long upstairs hallway she followed the butler along was equally impressive. The floor was of marble, which was cold beneath her worn soles, unlike the sunbaked stones at the entrance.

Mr. Leonard stopped at a closed door and opened it.

"Miss Catriona Fraiser," he announced, ushering her inside.

Catriona managed a small smile of thanks before walking into the enormous drawing room. There were several people already there, their faces unfamiliar, and all conversation ceased the moment she set foot inside. Many pairs of strange eyes now stared at her, and she felt instantly intimidated as she bobbed a curtsey in greeting.

She soon noticed that everyone was dressed in such fine attire that even the smallest item had probably cost more than her entire outfit, and was in far better shape too.

A short, middle-aged lady took it upon herself to speak first.

"Are you lost?" the woman demanded loudly, raising her eyebrows at Catriona. "The servant's quarters are situated *downstairs,* not up here."

Footsteps behind Catriona meant she didn't have a chance to respond, but she didn't dare turn around to see whose they were. Part of her wished she was lost and looking for the servant's quarters.

"I have invited Miss Fraiser to this meeting, Lady Spencer," a male voice said, and she recognized it as Mr. Dilworth's.

Thank the Lord he had arrived in time to keep Catriona from being further embarrassed . . . or embarrassing herself.

"Invited her?" Lady Spencer drawled, looking Catriona up and down disdainfully. "What business can a servant girl have here at the reading of my brother's will?"

"If you would calm yourself, Lady Spencer, I shall reveal all when I begin the reading," Mr. Dilworth said. "Now, since everyone is here, Miss Fraiser, please take a seat. We shall begin very shortly."

Mr. Dilworth moved past her to take a seat at a desk in the corner of the room. While he settled his papers, Catriona looked around her and took a seat at the back of the assembled company, trying to be as unobtrusive as she could. Still, it was now clear to her that the others had no idea of what she was doing there either.

"Please, enough of the dramatics, Mr. Dilworth," another woman spoke up. "Let's get on with it. Surely, there's no need for all this mystification.

The speaker was older than Lady Spencer but no less impressively dressed.

"If you would please wait just a moment more, Lady Beaumore," Mr. Dilworth said. "I am sure everyone, Miss Fraiser included, is wondering why she is here today. As soon as I have opened this will, I shall explain it all. But I ask for just a moment longer, to be sure I have it all properly prepared."

A hush settled over the room. Catriona dared not ask anyone else what they thought she was there for. And no one seemed interested in asking her either. She'd honestly thought she was being farmed out as servant to the family, hence Lady Spencer's reaction. But then, Mr. Dilworth's words at the orphanage returned to her.

*My presence is specifically required here. He made that plain. But whatever for?*

Mr. Dilworth suddenly cleared his throat, abruptly puncturing the heavy silence in the room.

"I now read directly from the will of the late Viscount Beaumore, and I ask that you all remain quiet until I have finished reading this specific portion of the will. And I quote, 'My dearest family, I do not know when this will shall be read to you all, but I do know one thing: I have kept a secret that I refuse to take to the grave with me. Before I fell ill here, I had no intentions of revealing it. In my youth, I married a young woman named Elspeth Fraiser."

Silence fell again as Mr. Dilworth looked over the page at everyone, but particularly at Catriona. She felt heat rising in her cheeks. Fraiser. Her last name was Fraiser.

"That marriage came about because Elspeth was a wonderful woman. A year later, she gave birth to a baby girl, whom we named Catriona. Sadly, Elspeth passed away shortly thereafter. I was in no condition to raise our daughter alone. So, I sent her away to an orphanage, never to know of her family. Until I fell ill and became full of regret. Thus, it is my intention that with this new will, I leave my entire estate and fortune to my daughter, wherever she may be, and under whatever name she uses today."

He put the paper down.

"A daughter?" Lady Spencer frowned deeply as she spoke. "And we are to believe it has taken six months to read my brother's will because of this?"

"Yes, Lady Spencer. I have spent those six months searching for Miss Fraiser. You see, it is no happenstance that I waited until I had found Miss Fraiser to read that paragraph, and the will in its entirety." He looked at Catriona. "Miss Fraiser, my apologies for not saying anything yesterday of this, but I have proof that you are the single legitimate daughter of the late viscount."

A shocked silence filled the room, though some of the others turned to peer at her, disapproval on their faces.

Catriona stood up to walk across to Mr. Dilworth, to see the will herself. She didn't get far before her knees buckled underneath her and the whole room began tilting to one side.

"Miss Fraiser!"

A voice called her name, but she couldn't tell whose before everything around her faded to black.

The next thing Catriona knew was that she was laying on a soft bed in a lavishly decorated bedchamber. She realized she'd been moved from the drawing room to a bedchamber by someone—perhaps by some of the servants of the household. A young woman was sitting next to the bed.

"Oh, thank goodness you've awoken. You gave us all quite a scare. I'm Bridget, by the way, Lady Beaumore," the woman introduced herself. "My husband is the new viscount, but I suppose that's all new to you. We're just glad you're all right after that fright. Take all the time you need to rest. We can talk more in the morning."

Lady Beaumore smiled at her as she got up and left the room, quietly closing the door behind her.

Catriona wasn't about to argue. After what had happened in the drawing room, she thought the offer of a good night's rest was worth taking up, if only to avoid the others for a bit longer. With the sound of the door shutting behind Lady Beaumore, she laid back on the bed gratefully, her mind in whirl.

The legitimate daughter of a viscount . . . and he'd sent her to live in the orphanage?

She couldn't quite fathom it. However, if that was what the will said, then who was she to argue with it? It may not have anything to do with how she had actually ended up in the orphanage, but she had no way of knowing. She had been there since she could remember. Perhaps her father had originally entrusted her care to someone else?

But for now, she attempted to push all that aside and try to get some proper sleep. Her world had just turned upside down . . . and she wasn't going to get anywhere with no rest.

## Chapter Three

Catriona's dreams, which involved finding her own Prince Charming, were ended by a faint knock on the door to the bedchamber. "Come in," she said in a small voice, sitting up against the pillows. The door opened to admit Lady Beaumore and another young woman in the uniform of a maid, who hung back.

"Good morning, Catriona," Lady Beaumore said with a smile. "Mary here will see to all of your needs. Everything is probably a little . . . overwhelming for you just now, I'm sure."

"Yes, my lady. The will . . . yesterday . . . well, it was a great shock. I cannot believe I am to be an heiress. It is . . . something I could only have dreamed of, Lady Beaumore, if it is true."

"Oh, it is true, I assure you. And that means we're family now. Call me Bridget, please." The woman smiled. "I cannot promise things will be easy for any of us at first. But I think you and I shall become very good friends as time goes by. Now, I know you probably don't have much in the way of possessions—Mr. Dilworth had Mary bring up your trunk—so, I have brought this for you to wear today. I think it will fit you quite well."

Now, Catriona saw that Mary was holding a dress over her arm, along with some other items of clothing and a pair of embroidered slippers.

"I have several others you can wear while the modiste prepares a proper wardrobe for you, Catriona, but this ought to do for the day's activities," Bridget continued. "We can have alterations done if necessary. But in the meantime," she added, picking up the old orphanage dress from the back of a chair with her fingertips, "this will have to go. From now on, gray is not your color." She handed it to Mary, whose nose wrinkled as she dropped it on the floor by the wardrobe.

"I don't think it's anyone's color, my lady," Catriona said with a bitter laugh. "But thank you, Bridget, it is very kind of you to worry about me."

The woman nodded and left Catriona alone with Mary.

It didn't take long for Mary to help Catriona to slip into her new things. The gown wasn't as fancy as anything she might have expected Bridget to wear, but it was certainly fancier than anything she had ever worn before.

Once she had been properly laced into it, which made her catch her breath, and the fabric was smoothed out across her form, Mary declared her approval. Then, the maid showed Catriona the way from her bedchamber to the dining room.

As they drew closer, Catriona smelled something delicious. She soon realized the family was having breakfast, and she was to join them. That made sense. If she had grown up here as the daughter of the viscount, she would have breakfasted with them every day. *But now . . . I am the outsider.*

Mary didn't enter the drawing room with her, but she opened the door and smiled encouragingly as Catriona entered. The family looked up, nodding at her as a servant showed her to a seat.

"Good morning, Catriona," Bridget said, smiling at her.

"Good morning to you all," Catriona said shyly, looking at all the different foodstuffs arranged before her. Never had she seen such a table groaning with food! Besides, she was starving. She'd not had anything to eat the night before, and her anxiety over the reading of the will had robbed her of any appetite for much of yesterday and the night before.

To start, Catriona decided on toast. Thickly buttered, with marmalade.

"Well, now you have joined us," said the man at the head of the table, "I do believe it is time for some proper introductions."

Another man said, "My name is Anthony, and I believe you've met my wife, Bridget." He gestured at Bridget, who sat opposite him.

Catriona transferred her attention from her toast and nodded politely at them both.

It was Anthony who made the rest of the introductions. Catriona greeted everyone as they were introduced to her. How would she remember all their names? There was Eleanor, the dowager viscountess, who had been addressed as Lady Beaumont yesterday by Mr. Dilworth, she recalled. Margaret, addressed as Lady Spencer, was apparently her aunt. And finally, there was Hannah Mills—the dowager's youngest child.

Hannah's elder brother, William, was away on business, Catriona learned. He was a merchant, Hannah informed her. The dowager commented that it was nice to have breakfast with her family while her son was absent, as he often was. It kept her from feeling as if she was truly alone at home.

"And I assume you all know my name, but I suppose it wouldn't hurt to say it again. I'm Catriona," Catriona said as she picked up her toast and finally began eating.

She hadn't exactly expected any conversation that morning, as everyone was probably still taking in the news, like herself. But she wouldn't have been upset if they had attempted to learn more about how she had grown up. *Where I came by that gray dress is probably what the women are wondering, no doubt, especially when paired with such worn out shoes.*

As she cast a glance around the room, she couldn't help but notice the frown on Eleanor's face as she buttered her toast.

"You're in dire need of lessons on etiquette and decorum, Miss," she announced through pursed lips. "Wherever Chilton left you to be raised, it certainly has not done a job worthy of the daughter of a viscount."

Catriona couldn't help but blush in mortification as she struggled to swallow her toast. Eleanor's comment had made everyone turn to stare at her and the way she was eating it. Was there a wrong way to do it, then?

"Now, what Mr. Dilworth shared yesterday was a shock to us all, and I imagine it was a shock to Catriona more than any of us," Anthony chimed in. "We must all give her some time to take it all in. I'm sure once she's had some time to settle in and think about what this means for her, then she'll be ready for her etiquette and decorum lessons, Mother."

Catriona quietly appreciated Anthony standing up for her. He must have understood from her reaction that it was quite a shock indeed. Her worn-out clothing might have been the another giveaway, but that was something she didn't want to consider just then.

"I disagree," Margaret said, speaking as though Catriona wasn't there. "You are already married, Anthony, and thus you have forgotten how quickly the *ton* takes hold of new women. She must be presented at once. The *ton* will find out about her being Chilton's daughter soon enough, and we have no time to waste if we want to present her this Season."

Catriona worried she'd never finish the meal if they kept talking about how she was to live her life, without allowing her any say in the matter.

"I agree with Margaret," Eleanor said. "Catriona, you must prepare to be presented to the *ton*, and as soon as possible."

It took every muscle in her body to keep the toast down as Catriona attempted to imagine how many people would now be looking at her as part of High Society. Her every move would be scrutinized. Especially since she had not grown up in that world. She'd grown up an orphan, and she doubted there were many people of the *ton* who would be sympathetic to this difficult change she was having to make.

Around the table, it seemed Eleanor's words were accepted as fact, and the lull in conversation meant Catriona managed to choke down a small breakfast of buttered toast, scrambled eggs, and excellent, hot coffee to wash it all down. Sadly, she couldn't even appreciate the taste of the food which she had not had to prepare for herself. Not with everyone watching her, judging her—and finding her wanting.

"Excuse me," Catriona said, rising once she had finished her breakfast. "I am not feeling entirely well."

No one attempted to stop her when she left the room, though she was sure she heard a whisper that being presented to the *ton* had likely made her sick. She heard Anthony saying that there had been no need for the women to have frightened her by throwing her in at the deep end so quickly. But she was too far away to hear the response.

Once in her bedchamber, she excused Mary, who insisted Catriona ring for her if she needed her. Alone, Catriona sank into the chair by a bureau.

She rifled through the drawers until she found pen, ink, and paper, smoothing out the sheet before her. Though she could not entirely share her feelings with her newfound family, she knew Alice would be able to understand what she was thinking . . . and *why* she thought it.

For now, all Catriona wanted was to be back at the orphanage with her best friend.

*Dear Alice,*

*You would not believe the upset that has happened here at Beaumore Manor. Mr. Dilworth, the man who came to get me from the orphanage, is a solicitor who worked for the late Viscount Beaumore. Apparently, when the man fell ill, he rewrote his entire will to leave it all to his estranged daughter.*

*To me, Alice. Me. I cannot fathom being the daughter of a viscount, and I cannot help but wonder if it would have been better if he had kept his secret and gone to the grave with it. The Beaumont family are nice enough, but I feel so out of place.*

*Lady Spencer, who appears to be the eldest of the Beaumont siblings, is quite full of her own opinions. She actually believed I was lost when I first arrived, informing me that the servant's quarters were downstairs. I fully believe she might have dragged me down there herself if Mr. Dilworth hadn't told everyone that he had invited me to the will reading.*

*She and her mother, the Dowager Viscountess Beaumore, both believe I need to be taught perfect etiquette and decorum. And quickly too. They want to present me to the* ton *as soon as possible as the late viscount's daughter, since it seems the news will leak out sooner rather than later.*

*Please, do not share this news with anyone. If they ask, tell them I have gotten a maid's job elsewhere. I am not entirely sure what I want to do with my new station yet, and I would greatly appreciate having only you, and perhaps Mrs. Easton, knowing what brought me to Beaumore Manor.*

*Thankfully, there are those here who agree it is quite a shock to me. The current viscount, a young man named Anthony Beaumont, and his wife Lady Bridget have been kind in making sure I am comfortable in my new position in life. But I do not know who to trust.*

*After all, my manners are not those of an upper-class lady. This change is all very new and difficult. Is it wrong to wish I was back there with you at the orphanage, where my only worry for the day was where and when I was going to eat my lunch?*

*Please write back. You are perhaps the only person in the world who can truly understand how shocking all this is to me.*

*Your friend,*
*Catriona Fraiser*

Catriona didn't feel a need to change her name at the end of her letter to Alice. Furthermore, it would look as though only a servant was writing to her at the orphanage, which was for the best if she wanted to keep her secret.

Knowing she was to be trained as a lady, Catriona wasn't sure how to do anything but follow the advice of Bridget the day before—rest and adjust as best she could. There would be time for everything else as she grew used to her new surroundings. As Anthony had said, there would be plenty of time for her to learn all that was necessary.

So long as she didn't do anything for the time being to reveal herself to the *ton* as the late viscount's daughter, at least. That meant she'd probably be cooped up in Beaumore Manor—her new home—until she was ready to be presented to Society.

While it wasn't the worst situation in the world, she still found it hard to accept. *Instead of just taking things as they come, I should spend some time familiarizing myself with the manor. That might, at least, give me some clues as to what I've gotten into.*

So, she rang the bell to call for Mary, who duly arrived. Upon Mary's suggestion, Bridget was asked and agreed to join them for a small tour of the manor. That brought some comfort to Catriona. The Viscountess Beaumore had already shown herself to be quite understanding of the awkward situation Catriona found herself in. So far, she had done but help her adjust to the sudden change in her fortunes.

## Chapter Four

Hamish spent the next morning filling in his account ledgers. It was a normal routine for him as part of running a business. And in the wake of learning of his father's intense desire for him to marry Lady Josette Ashmore, it gave him something else to focus on.

As he closed the ledger, with all figures perfectly balanced, he decided to check his pocket watch for the time. He'd removed the clock from his Mayfair townhouse's study because it always made him feel as though there was too much ticking going on to distract him. Even now, he could hear the faint ticking of the pocket watch as the hands turned with each passing second.

That was more than enough to tell him that time was moving on, and that he had to move with it to make sure all was kept under control.

Upon glancing at the watch, he was more than a little shocked to realize it was almost time to meet Anthony for fencing and drinks. He was sure that, whatever had happened the day before with the late viscount's solicitor, Anthony would have plenty to tell him. That only made him more eager to see his friend.

Snatching up his coat, Hamish left the study, making sure to shut and lock the door on his way out. Though no one else would be coming into the house while he was away, it was a habit he had retained from his time in the Far East. One never knew who might be tempted to poke about.

The carriage set off for Beaumore Manor once again, rolling through the gates of his small estate on the outskirts of London, which his parents had found for him as a home on his return to England. It was handy for attending the Season's many events. When he eventually married, he would bring his wife here, too. *Hopefully, it won't be Lady Josette.*

Lady Josette Ashmore. She was indeed a beautiful woman, with lustrous black hair that framed her face becomingly, and striking blue eyes that made her hair seem all the darker. But he was not at all sure she was the one he wanted to spend the rest of his life with.

The way she had acted at the dinner table upon his arrival back in London was what had tipped him off to *that*. He had not found much to say to her but noticed that she was not bothered about it in the slightest. She had been more than happy to prattle on about the latest fashions, the juiciest gossip and rumors, and which scandals had ruined whom.

Rumors her family likely started, Hamish thought as the carriage continued to roll along the roads of Mayfair. The Ashmore family had a bit of a reputation for ruining people they didn't like, but no one in Town could ever quite prove it. It was all rumor and speculation, no better than the gossip they themselves spread at others' expense. But it was believable to him simply because Hamish knew the Ashmore family and his father all too well.

They would do anything to get what they wanted. The thought of being under pressure from his father to make sure he married Lady Josette proved it.

His thoughts were interrupted by his arrival at Beaumore Manor. Hamish descended the carriage, was welcomed inside, and made his way up the stairs to meet Anthony. His thoughts of Lady Josette were quickly replaced by his excitement at fencing again with his old friend.

He wondered if Anthony had gotten any better at the sport since he himself had been away in the Far East. If he was to believe Anthony, his friend had been far too busy recently to engage in such pastimes, but he still liked it. Hamish hoped it was true. Hamish had experienced much of the same abroad, struggling to make time for the sport among all the business meetings and other exotic activities he had to choose between.

The Beaumont family butler, Leonard, opened the door for him.

"Ah, Lord Milington, what a pleasure. His lordship says you are to go up to the study."

"Thank you, Leonard," Hamish said as he stepped into the hallway, handed Leonard his hat, and set off up the stairs. As he reached the first landing, he heard two female voices floating up from the hallway below and glanced over his shoulder.

Viscountess Beaumore had entered the hallway followed by another young woman. Hamish frowned as he looked at the other woman for a moment longer than perhaps was appropriate. He could have sworn he had seen her before. She wore a pale blue dress that set off her bright blue eyes. Damn! Where had he seen them before?

"Ah, Lord Milington, what a pleasure to see you today," Viscountess Beaumore said, looking up and meeting his eyes. Hamish retraced his steps downstairs to the hall, intrigued. "May I introduce Miss Beaumont, the daughter of the late Viscount Beaumore?"

Hamish offered a bow of respect to the young lady and smiled at her. But Miss Beaumont simply stood there, staring at him, her blue eyes wide. He found it rather odd. Did the young woman not know how to curtsey or greet a person properly? And how was it that he had never heard of her existence until that moment? Miss Beaumont, after all, was a viscount's daughter . . .

Before Hamish or Miss Beaumont could say anything more, Leonard returned.

"Ah! Lord Milington, how fortuitous. His lordship requests that you meet him in the *piste* instead," he said.

Hamish nodded. "Of course. I know the way." He turned once more to the ladies. "I am summoned, it seems. Excuse me. Enjoy your day."

He gave another bow before heading to the rear of the mansion, still trying to remember where he had seen Miss Beaumont before.

It wasn't long, however, before that thought had perished as he drew his rapier to fight Anthony in a short fencing duel. The fencing didn't last long, however, as Anthony found himself tiring far too quickly. Perhaps living in the Far East and having to walk long distances to accomplish anything had helped Hamish in this endeavor.

"I met Miss Beaumont while waiting for you, Anthony," Hamish said as his friend regained his breath. "She is quite something. Is that what the meeting with the solicitor was all about yesterday?"

"Oh, that's not even the half of it, Hamish," Anthony panted. "Now, how about those drinks I mentioned?"

Hamish was more than a little taken aback by the way his friend suddenly switched the topic from Miss Beaumont. But he was more than happy to sit down. Perhaps Anthony was using this as a convenient way to get out of another round of fencing, but Hamish had to admit that he was more than a little curious about the young woman.

"Catriona—or as you met her, Miss Beaumont—as grown up in an orphanage," Anthony said once drinks had been served, and they were completely alone. "Mr. Dilworth spent six months tracking her down after Father's death. Seems he had married a young Scottish woman a year before Catriona was born . . . and did not think he was up to the task of taking care of a child all alone."

"Was it the illness that convinced him he had made a bad decision at that point in his life?"

Hamish took a sip of his whiskey, but he was more interested in the story than the sharp bite of the alcohol.

"It seems so. She's been left not only a vast fortune but Beaumore Manor and several other unentailed properties too," Anthony said. "She's been overwhelmed the last couple of days. Bridget seems to have taken her under her wing, thankfully, as everyone else insists that she needs to be presented to the *ton* immediately. It's going to be quite a busy time around here . . ."

"And where does that leave you? I thought you and Bridget were to inherit the manor."

"We shall be staying here for now, yes," Anthony answered, "but where we shall go after that all depends on what Catriona wants. It's her manor, after all, and we shall not stand on ceremony if she were to wish us to leave the house at once. We can always go elsewhere. She might wish to entail one of the other properties to us, or we could simply find a conveniently situated manor of our own."

"Then, is she the one in the gray dress from yesterday?" Hamish raised an eyebrow.

If that was the case, he could hardly believe how quickly Bridget and the others in the house had managed to bring the girl into the fold. She was not entirely ready to be presented to the *ton*, Hamish believed, but she certainly was starting to look the part.

"Yes. Actually, now I think about it, she did arrive as I sent you away yesterday. Did you see her on the steps, then?" Anthony asked.

Hamish decided it was doing his friend no favors to keep that story from him. He shared how he had kept a young woman in a gray dress from falling on her face on the steps. It appeared to him as if the young woman had been distracted by something and tripped.

"She stared at me rather unnervingly," he finished.

"Miss Beaumont may have been staring at you, but that's easy to explain," Anthony said. "Who knows what kind of men were around her at the orphanage? She may have been simply taken aback by how richly dressed you were yesterday, or by the manor itself. It's funny, isn't it? You saw her going inside the house, when she would not have known this manor actually belongs to her."

"She looked entirely lost. She couldn't even find words to say anything when I asked if she was all right after she tripped. Just stared at me. The woman escorting her, I assume she was from the orphanage, interrupted us before the girl could say anything, and I was quite upset about it. She looked as if she was about to find her tongue and introduce herself to me." Hamish laughed. "Then again, I suppose it would not have been appropriate."

"I don't think she would have known or cared about that," Anthony said. "She probably just wanted to thank you."

"You wound me, Anthony, you wound me," Hamish teased.

They both laughed. Anthony finished the last of his whiskey, and Hamish took another small sip if his own.

"Well, I do suppose that would explain why she only stared at me some more when I was introduced to her properly by Bridget," Hamish now said. "She wouldn't have known to curtsey to me before that."

"If anyone else was here, you might have ruined a reputation before it began, Hamish."

Anthony gave him a stern look.

"There's a reason I said it in front of you, and you alone," Hamish said. "I do not wish to harm a reputation that has not yet had a chance to start. That is not *my* business, after all. Speaking of business, would this be a good time to talk about our business venture, or has the arrival of Miss Beaumont made that difficult for you?"

"Well, it seems the rest of my relatives and Bridget have her in hand, and I do not know entirely what she needs," Anthony said. "For now, I suppose, we are in the clear."

# Chapter Five

Catriona sat in the drawing room with Bridget, her knee bouncing slightly beneath her skirts. They were awaiting the arrival of the dowager, Lady Spencer, and Mrs. Mills. Catriona felt that the dowager and Mrs. Mills had the best in mind for her; it was Lady Spencer's impending arrival that had her knee bouncing.

Lady Spencer's remarks the day before at breakfast, as well as those she had made when she had first arrived at Beaumore Manor, had made Catriona feel small. Before arriving at Beaumore Manor, she had thought it impossible to make someone feel smaller than Mrs. Easton made the older orphans feel. She'd learned very quickly that that was not the case.

It appeared to be Lady Spencer's specialty.

Bridget put a hand on Catriona's, as if she had realized she was agitated.

"It'll be all right. Do not let Margaret affect you." Bridget offered a soft smile. "I had a hard time being accepted into this family, too. Purely because my father is involved in trade and was not well-off from birth." She took in a deep breath.

"She has a talent for making people feel unworthy, Lady Spencer does," Catriona muttered.

This actually drew a stifled laugh from Bridget. Upon hearing it, she looked to the other young woman, and found her struggling to maintain her composure for just a moment before composing herself. It made Catriona a bit jealous. That was the kind of thing that took years to learn how to do properly; she didn't think she'd be able to learn how to do it in just a few weeks, as everyone had been hinting that she'd have to.

"The best thing you can do around Margaret is hold your head high and keep your dignity about you," Bridget warned. "It only takes her a while to warm up to someone who is new to the family, especially when they have not come from the upper-class themselves. To go from an orphan who knows nothing of our world to the daughter of the late viscount is a hard change. She would not understand, as she has had money and comfort since birth."

"Thank you, Bridget."

"The dowager Lady Spencer and Mrs. Mills have arrived, Viscountess Beaumore."

Leonard's voice interrupted the rather heartfelt conversation Catriona was having with Bridget.

Bridget nodded and excused herself from the room to go and arrange the tea for the afternoon with the cook. This left Catriona alone with the dowager Eleanor, Lady Spencer, and Mrs. Mills. Part of Catriona wished she had been able to go and arrange the tea. But part of her knew that Bridget had gone because Catriona would have come back with a tea tray in hand and served them all like a maid, doing everything to avoid talking to Lady Spencer.

Then again, perhaps it was better that Bridget had been the one to leave. If what she had said was true and Lady Spencer simply needed to see that Catriona was growing into her role as the daughter of the late viscount in Society, then it would not be seemly of her to be the one serving the tea—despite it being something she knew how to do.

"Ah, how lovely to see you again, Catriona," Eleanor said.

"And you, Eleanor," Catriona said, "Lady Spencer, Mrs. Mills."

"Please, it's Dowager Viscountess," Lady Spencer corrected her. "Unless the dowager has given you permission to call her that."

"Enough with the formalities, Margaret," the dowager said. "We need not keep Catriona bound to such things when it is only family at tea. After all, she is my only grandchild."

Catriona gulped hard at that. That single fact meant there was a lot for her to learn to make this woman proud of her once she was presented to the *ton.* And it was not going to be an easy feat to learn all the rules of behavior in just a few weeks, or even a few months. All the other young ladies would have had *years* to learn it all naturally, and from when they were small, when it was drummed into them and they never forgot it.

The dowager then turned to Catriona.

"Please, Eleanor is fine when it is just family," she said. "Margaret is just a little too prim sometimes when it comes to these things. That said, it is imperative that you are prepared as soon as possible to be presented to the *ton*. To do that, you will have to learn how to properly address those of title around you."

Catriona quietly thanked the heavens when a housemaid came in carrying a tea tray. Tea was now served, though Bridget was nowhere in sight to alleviate some of the pressure on Catriona. She only wanted to feel she was doing things right. Bridget offered that without making her feel like an idiot for not knowing how to act like a viscount's daughter in company.

As she took her tea, Catriona could feel Lady Spencer sizing her up. Part of her again wished she could have been the housemaid who had now slipped out of the room after serving tea. She could be in the kitchen now, discussing plans for dinner with Alice, or she could have been anywhere else.

Anywhere but under the ever-watchful eye of this judgmental woman.

"You'll need a lady's maid capable of transforming you into what Society expects of a viscount's daughter," Lady Spencer finally said. "I do happen to know of a young lady who would be more than happy to fill the position, if you need help finding one."

"Thank you, Lady Spencer, but I have already taken care of the lady's maid position. Should the arrangement fall through, I'll gladly take up your offer," Catriona replied.

It was not entirely true, but she did have someone in mind for the position. The last few days had been far too tiring to actually pen a letter to Alice asking her. She might refuse, but the mere thought of having her friend at the manor with her was comforting.

"That's certainly one less thing to worry about, and I would think that's a good thing, Margaret," Mrs. Mills chimed in.

It appeared that in matters of etiquette and decorum, Mrs. Mills deferred to Lady Spencer and her mother. She was not entirely surprised to learn that, considering Mrs. Mills had married a merchant, she no longer mixed so much with the *ton*.

"Well, now we have had our tea, I do believe that it is time for you to have some proper lessons on how to address everyone," Eleanor told Catriona. "This will be among the easiest things you'll have to learn, but as the news spreads, people will come to see you. They will want to be introduced, and it is important that you know how to introduce yourself, how to address them, and how to curtsey."

They started with the curtsey, since that was the easiest to learn. Everyone did their best curtsey for Catriona. Though it looked easy, when Catriona first attempted it, she found herself wobbling uncontrollably. Lady Spencer stifled a laugh, but it was clear that no one else was laughing at her clumsy attempt.

Eleanor offered Catriona some advice on how to place her feet, and Catriona tried again. The next try went better. With a little more practice, Catriona had mastered the curtsey, which seemed to please everyone.

That gave Catriona the confidence she needed to start learning how to properly address everyone. That portion of the afternoon felt like a never-ending lecture from Lady Spencer, however, as the woman would immediately point out Catriona's many mistakes. A viscount was a lord, yes, but how one addressed him in conversation entirely depended on how close one was to him personally. The same went for a viscountess, Catriona's equal in status.

It was the earls, the barons, the dukes, and everyone above her that gave her trouble. There was no simple solution. She simply had to remember not only their title, but the title attached to their land and not their last name. Some situations were easier to remember than others. For instance, Beaumont was the last name of the Viscount Beaumore, but often the title did not match the family name at all.

By the time the women had finished with her for the evening and sent her off to her room for the night, Catriona was thoroughly exhausted. Bridget had never entirely returned to the room, but she had come in to see what kind of progress was being made. Catriona wondered how young girls took to all the lessons they had to learn. She would never catch up with them, but they had grown up with it.

When Catriona did finally return to her room, she half thought about just falling face first into the bed and not bothering to change into her nightclothes. Dinner and lessons were done for the day, and she had no reason to go anywhere else.

However, she knew there was one thing that she had to do first before going to bed. She had to write to Alice again. She wanted to be sure she had at least attempted to fill the position of lady's maid before allowing Lady Spencer to do it for her. If her guess was right, Lady Spencer would probably hire a lady's maid who was just as critical of Catriona as she was. That was the *last* thing Catriona wanted!

Especially since she already felt entirely unworthy of her new role, thanks to Lady Spencer.

So, she sat down at the desk to write to Alice, resolving to do so and change into her nightclothes later, with Mary's help.

*Dear Alice,*

*You would not believe what a long day I have just had, but that is not the reason for me writing to you again. I know my other letter was long, but this one is probably going to be just as long. I've spent the entire day learning all the noble titles and how to properly address everyone. And how to curtsey. Would you believe there is actually a wrong way to curtsey and it doesn't come naturally to everyone?*

*I wouldn't have guessed!*

*But the reason I am writing this letter is not to discuss any of that, not really. I am actually writing because Lady Spencer—my aunt, apparently—says I must have a lady's maid. She has someone in mind, but I would rather find someone myself, for she is very critical of me. I wonder if it's because I was raised in an orphanage or because she didn't like my mother. If she even knew my mother . . .*

*Would you like to be my lady's maid? I cannot guarantee that you'll feel any less judged and unworthy than I do. But perhaps it won't be so bad for you, since you will be fulfilling a role that Lady Spencer would have deemed me fit for upon my first arrival here at Beaumore Manor.*

*I do so hope you'll say yes. It'd be nice to have someone else in the manor who understands what troubles me about all of this, and I think you'd have the best knowledge in that regard. I don't exactly know what I'd have to do to arrange transportation and everything for you, but I'm sure as soon as I mention you're interested, we'd be able to do something to get you up here.*

*I do so miss you, Alice. How is everything going at the orphanage? Are you still in charge of mopping the floors every day? How is that going? Has Mrs. Easton said anything about where I went to the rest of the girls in the orphanage, or have you all been left to wonder what happened to me? Hurry and write back!*

*Your friend,*
*Miss Catriona Beaumont*

It felt so odd to sign her name as Catriona Beaumont at the bottom of the letter instead of Catriona Fraiser, but the ladies thought she had better get into the habit. Even Anthony had suggested that the sooner she started using her proper name in correspondence the better. It would at least lend more credence to everything.

She still put Catriona Fraiser in the return address, though, simply to make sure that Mrs. Easton understood who was writing to Alice.

## Chapter Six

Once again seated in the study of his Mayfair townhouse, Hamish reflected on the woman he had been properly introduced to only two days ago. She was quite intriguing, if he had anything to admit about his feelings towards her. So far, at least.

To have grown up in an orphanage and now be told she was the heir to a fortune, a manor, and a title . . . he could hardly believe how much trouble she would have understanding the change. Yet Miss Beaumont had seemed to take it all in her stride, and he thought he had clearly caught her attention.

What caught *his* attention was that Miss Beaumont had not curtseyed to him both times when they had met, not on the steps when she'd tripped or in the hallway. Knowing now that she probably hadn't known how or when to curtsey, he could excuse it. But what if she'd deliberately 'forgotten' in his case? Judging by the way she had stared at him, she seemed particularly taken by his features. He couldn't lie to himself and say it wasn't nice to know that someone was intrigued by him—if that's what it was.

But what he couldn't abide was knowing there was nothing he could do about it just then.

She had not yet been presented to the *ton*, and as much as he wanted to throw all caution to the wind and approach her, he knew Anthony too well to do that. His friend wanted to see Miss Beaumont succeed in her new station in life. Beginning a courtship with him now would only start rumors flying. He didn't want to be a reason for the *ton* to talk about her in a bad way.

He had no doubt that the Ashmore family would be the ones to start those rumors, if it became necessary for their aims.

His thoughts about how to get around the tricky situation were interrupted by the sound of the door opening. His butler entered the room with a letter for him on a silver tray.

"This has just arrived from your father, Lord Milington," he said, bowing before proffering the tray.

"Thank you."

Hamish took the letter from the tray and then dismissed him softly with a wave of his hand.

As he started to open the letter, he knew it could only refer to one of several things—it was from his father, after all. His father never really had anything good to say to him in his letters. Indeed, Hamish reflected, and it was through his frequent letters that his father had hoped to maintain some form of control over Hamish in the Far East.

That hadn't exactly worked out because the two societies were so vastly different. But now Hamish was back in London, the method would likely be more effective in getting him to do what his father wanted.

He groaned upon reading that the letter was simply a reminder that they had all been invited to a garden tea party—being hosted at Ashington Manor. He wanted to avoid the Ashmore family as much as possible. But his father—in the hopes that Hamish would eventually court and then marry Lady Josette—was clearly devoting much time to finding ways to throw the pair together, whether Hamish liked it or not.

So far, the duke was winning. In order to keep the peace, Hamish knew he would have to attend the tea party. In truth, he'd forgotten all about it. A garden tea party had been the last thing on his mind since meeting the intriguing Miss Beaumont.

Only a few hours later, he was stepping out of his carriage at Ashington Manor. As he alighted, he realized another carriage had pulled up behind his. When his parents stepped out of it, he internally groaned. What bad luck! He had hoped they would not have arrived yet, so he could greet the Ashmore family before quietly slipping away before his father had even realized he'd been there.

That was no longer an option, and Hamish quietly resigned himself to another night of conversation with Lady Josette, if he could even call her prattling on about her latest achievements a conversation.

"Good evening, Mother, Father," Hamish said, bowing respectfully when they noticed him.

They approached him, and he noticed his father had a smile on his face.

"What a pleasure to see you, Hamish," his father said. "I was honestly a little worried you would not come. After all, it is in our family's best interest that you marry Lady Josette. This is a perfect opportunity to start laying the foundations for the courtship that will lead to that."

Hamish only nodded before they walked inside. He didn't dare say anything to give his father a reason to believe he was not going to play by the rules that had been laid out for him tonight. *It's only one night.* Hopefully, Lady Josette would do enough talking for them both, and he could simply daydream while seeming to be paying attention to her.

It had worked at dinner the last time, after all.

The butler escorted them out to the rose garden, and Hamish was not at all surprised to see he was conveniently seated beside Lady Josette at the tea table. *Father and Lord Ashmore are probably working in tandem to put this marriage together . . .*

Lady Josette batted her eyelashes at him as he greeted the family.

"What a wonderful night it is, Lord Milington," she said. She looked up at him, her eyes bright. "A pleasure to see you again so soon."

"Indeed," Hamish said noncommittally.

The conversation soon changed to Lady Josette telling him all about what she had been up to, just as he had expected. She talked about having learned another tune on the pianoforte, and even offered to play it for him sometime. As much as Hamish didn't want to pay her any attention, there was no other recourse for him at the table. The women made small talk, while his father and Lord Ashmore spoke only about business, as always.

Ironically, Lady Josette's achievements *were* the most interesting thing at the table. That was, until the countess shifted the topic of conversation among the rest of the ladies.

"I've heard there is a new lady to be presented to the *ton* this Season," the countess said. "Apparently, the late Viscount Beaumore has a daughter. And she grew up in an *orphanage*, of all places. Can you imagine seeing her ready for the *ton* in just one Season?"

Lady Josette actually laughed, and her younger sister only shook her head.

"It takes years of grooming, *training*, to present an unwedded woman to the *ton*," Lady Josette spoke up. "I cannot believe anyone could think she will be ready within a season. After all, someone from an orphanage will struggle to fit in amongst the *ton*!"

The other ladies snickered, and Hamish clenched his jaw. It was not right of them to be talking about Miss Beaumont so rudely without even knowing her. From what little he understood of the situation, she was doing her best to adjust. Of course, there would be bumps in the road along the way; it could not happen overnight. But was it so wrong of Miss Beaumont to want to try and be part of her new life instead of continuing to live as if ignorant of her good fortune?

"What gentleman would want to marry such a lady, if not for her money?" Lady Josette continued to deride Miss Beaumont.

And Hamish struggled not to protest.

"The man who marries her will have a tough time turning her into a lady the *ton* will accept, that's for certain," Lady Rosalie Ashmore said. "Why did the late Viscount Beaumore not want to raise her?"

"Whatever the reason," the countess said, "you can be certain of one thing, girls. She is not your competition. If a man goes after her, he is not worthy of you, either of you. Do you understand me? You ought to be looking for the gentlemen who know that it is the way you are brought up and not a newfound fortune that make a real lady."

Lady Josette and her younger sister agreed with their mother, nodding vigorously.

A few of the other ladies present gave their opinions on the new Miss Beaumont, but Hamish was not happy with any of them. How could they judge her so harshly when they hadn't even met her yet?

None of them had seen the way her eyes had widened upon seeing the manor for the very first time, as he had. They hadn't seen how out of place she had obviously felt being in that house, but he had. More importantly, none of them had taken the time to go and properly meet her, all waiting for her to be presented to the *ton* before they called on her—no doubt half hoping she would entertain them all by committing some terrible faux pas.

He thought that the worst crime of all, waiting for her to make her debut rather than befriending her and attempting to bring her into the fold beforehand, making her life a little easier. *Of course, it's going to be difficult for her to adjust to this new life. She grew up in an orphanage, and that's no easy feat in itself.*

Hamish had heard horror stories of some of those orphanages turning women away when they reached an eligible age, shoving them out onto the streets in hopes they'd find work or marry, so their bed would then be available for a younger child who might actually find a home.

Regardless of Hamish's thoughts on the subject, he refused to add to the gossip confronting him.

Until Lady Josette turned to him.

"You must be over at the Beaumore Manor quite a bit, my lord, being good friends with Viscount Beaumore," she said. "What do you think of this Miss Beaumont? Is she a lady worthy of the *ton*, or will she fail in her endeavor to adjust to her new life?"

"I have no opinion on the matter, Lady Josette," Hamish said dryly. "Whether or not she succeeds is not up to her, anyway.

If I were to believe what I've heard at this table, it is up to all of you to decide whether or not she fails. And she's already failed by your standards, I gather."

"We are merely saying that it won't be easy for her to succeed," the countess said, seeming a little flustered by his censure. "But I would not be surprised if she finds the lifestyle far too restricting compared to what she's used to. She's used to having more freedom to approach people as she pleases, working, having a busier life in general. I do not doubt she will miss doing certain things herself."

"I hear Lady Spencer mistook her for a new servant at the manor when she first arrived," Lady Rosalie said. "Servants talk. And when the gossip includes a lady being mistaken for one of them, they talk even louder. Can you imagine? A lady like that being presented to the *ton* in a single Season and succeeding at it? Preposterous!"

Hamish took a sip of his tea to quell his rising anger. So, she had limited time to prepare for the Season, but they had no way of knowing how well she would perform. And did they not think it natural for Miss Beaumont to initially assume she might have been hired as a new servant at the manor until she had been told otherwise? Clearly not, or they didn't care to acknowledge it.

Thankfully, he didn't have to listen to the gossip much longer, for the evening soon drew to a close. As Hamish got into his carriage, he decided to warn Anthony that there was already talk of Miss Beaumont in Town. She'd have to be properly presented sooner rather than later if they wanted it to go well, and especially before the Ashmore family could further poison the well.

# Chapter Seven

Two days after writing to Alice to ask if she would like to be her lady's maid, Catriona found herself in a spacious upstairs room near her bedchamber. She stood as still as she could as she was circled by the modiste, Lady Spencer, the dowager, and Lady Beaumore, who vied with one another in advising her what to wear. It was all very confusing, being posed this way and that like a doll, with a bewildering array of fabrics, trimmings, laces, buttons, and other fripperies being thrust at her by the modiste.

It was overwhelming. At the orphanage, her only option had been the plain, gray dress. That was all Mrs. Easton was willing to give the women. And now Catriona was seeing all of these other possibilities, she was not surprised. Gray didn't show the dirt.

"I feel she looks best in white," Lady Spencer continued. "She has such a complexion for it, and what other lady of the *ton* has a completely white wardrobe? No one, that's who. We want to make a statement with her, yes?"

"Lady Spencer, I am not entirely sure I would be able to keep a white wardrobe clean," Catriona said. "Isn't white rather difficult to keep clean, madam?"

She looked to the modiste, hoping for some help.

"Yes, and while white certainly suits Miss Beaumont, there are plenty of other pale colors which are just as flattering, so I suggest a combination of the two," the modiste said, smiling at Catriona. "White is hard to keep clean. If there are spills, say, it may mean having to replace clothing more frequently, which can be expensive."

"I don't understand why you're so worried about spilling things," Lady Spencer said, frowning at the woman. "Catriona hasn't spilled a thing yet!"

"Margaret," Eleanor said, "I agree with the modiste. If we put her in all white all the time, people will grow bored with seeing her. Pastels would look absolutely lovely on you, too, Catriona."

"Thank you," Catriona said. "Anything, as long as it's not gray."

"I agree with the dowager viscountess," the modiste spoke up. "Pastels would look gorgeous with your skin tone, Miss Beaumont, and I believe a pale blue would bring out those blue eyes of yours even more than white."

Lady Spencer huffed at that, but she finally relented about the white wardrobe. Catriona was relieved to hear it. She was actually quite happy to be wearing colors that wouldn't stain so easily. She said nothing about it then, but at the orphanage, she had stained at least two gray dresses by spilling tea. It would be awful if she did that with one of her lovely new ones.

Bridget had been the first to suggest pastels for Catriona, but she had stepped out for a moment before the current discussion had gotten to its height because Anthony had needed her opinion on something.

"Are we including pastels?" Bridget asked as she finally returned.

"Yes, my lady, and I do believe this blue suits her perfectly," the modiste said, holding up a pale blue swatch of fabric.

"Oh, it's lovely," Catriona breathed, eyeing it.

"You're right," Bridget said.

With the colors picked and Catriona having been finally able to get her way on some small things, the ladies went to the drawing room and tea was served. As she sipped her tea, Catriona silently admitted to herself that the more she learned about what was expected of her, the more she wanted to return to the orphanage. Having had no reply from Alice yet, she could only hope her friend would come.

"Something will have to be done about the way you style your hair, too, Catriona," Lady Spencer said. "That chignon is a practical style, but it does nothing for your face!"

"Margaret's right," Eleanor spoke up. "You have such a pretty face. That chignon so tightly drawn only puckers it. Why don't you let one of us curl your hair, or have your lady's maid curl it?"

"Because my lady's maid . . ."

Catriona stopped when the butler knocked and was admitted to the room.

He bowed, looking at Catriona. "A Miss Brown has arrived for you, Miss Beaumont," he said.

Her heart soaring, Catriona jumped up and hurried out of the room to the hall. There, standing looking lost, a small trunk by her side, was Alice! She flung herself into her arms, and Alice hugged her back, both of them laughing with joy.

"You are here! How wonderful. Thank you for coming. I'm so glad to see you, Alice!" Catriona said, grinning at Alice when they finally pulled apart.

"And I'm so glad to be here. This is a great opportunity for me, Catriona. I should be thanking you," Alice told her, eyes twinkling and filling Catriona with happiness. "What a beautiful manor. Is it really yours now?" Alice asked, looking around her in wonder.

"Yes, it's mine . . . and it'll be our home now too."

Alice shook her head and laughed lightly. "I can hardly believe it. What a change from the orphanage . . ."

Catriona chuckled and nodded. "I know—" she began, but footsteps stopped her from saying anything more.

"Catriona! You do not just get up and leave your guests like that when hosting a tea," Lady Spencer chided, poking her head out from the drawing room. "You must excuse yourself first. Where are your manners?"

The scolding caused Catriona's cheeks to flush. Recognizing the voice of authority, Alice pulled away from her and stood a few steps away, eyes downcast.

"Is this is your lady's maid, then?" Lady Spencer gave Alice a good look up and down. "She'll do, I suppose. We'll have to see how good she is at making you fashionable!" Her head disappeared back into the room.

"Come on, I'll show you my rooms and you can rest, but I have to go back into tea with them for a little while. I'll be as quick as I can," she told Alice. They took her trunk and went quickly up the stairs together.

With Alice safely installed Catriona's chambers and Catriona returning to the tea table for the best part of another hour, she was grateful when the gathering broke up and she could join her friend at last.

She found Alice in the small connecting room where she would sleep.

"This is so comfy," she said, wriggling luxuriously and making Catriona laugh again. "I think I shall like it here."

"And I shall love having you here. Now, what about a little tour? I hardly know my way around yet, but I can show you some of it. Then, I suppose, you must meet the other servants."

Off they went, but Catriona soon realized she was quite exhausted, and she could tell Alice was too, having come such a long way. They returned to the bedchamber and got themselves ready for bed, with Alice helping her out of her dress. For the first time, she didn't bother summoning Mary. They talked for a while, but then Alice went off to her new room, and soon, both were fast asleep.

The next morning, Alice stood behind Catriona as she sat at the vanity, looking in the mirror.

"Lady Spencer says the chignon I always wear is unbecoming. You're so good at styling hair, Alice. Will you do something different that will make me look nice?"

"Of course, I have something in mind already," Alice said and began working on Catriona's long locks. The new style began to take shape, and when Catriona inspected her reflection, she was pleased.

"It already looks much better," she said, smiling into the mirror.

As Alice worked, the girls chatted about their new lives.

"I'm so thankful to leave the orphanage," Alice said as she pinned up some stray tresses of Catriona's hair flatteringly. "It was rather depressing without you there."

"Well . . . I'm not sure that it'll be much better here, Alice," Catriona said. "This last week has been so overwhelming for me. There were times when . . . when I wished I was back at the orphanage."

With a loud gasp, Alice actually stopped working to stare at her friend in the mirror.

"You cannot be serious, Catriona . . . can you?" Alice raised her brows in shock. "This is . . . this is something you and I both *dreamed* of when we were at the orphanage. We were talking just the day before you left about what it might have been like to grow up somewhere like this."

"I know, but Alice, I'm worried. My biggest fear . . ."

Catriona let out a deep sigh as Alice resumed working on her hair.

". . .my biggest fear is that I'll fail and be a disappointment to the Beaumont family name. We know I didn't grow up in this environment. There's so much that I'm expected to remember all of a sudden, and I'm struggling to remember even how to address everyone correctly, even in my immediate family! I haven't even been given permission to address any of them, except for the Dowager Viscountess and the current Viscountess Beaumore, by their first names yet." Catriona stared her friend's reflection in the eyes. "There's so much to worry about."

Alice again paused in her work and placed a comforting hand on Catriona's shoulder, squeezing it softly.

"Practice makes perfect, Catriona. Besides . . . you worry too much," Alice said. "I'm sure that the feeling of being overwhelmed will soon wear off, and you'll be able to practice everything you need to in good time. In fact, I'm sure you'll be a *great* success. And you'll prove to be a wonderful addition to the Beaumont family. I know it."

"Really?"

"Not only that," Alice declared, "but I *know* the *ton* will love you too."

Catriona smiled as Alice finished styling her hair for the day.

"Thank you for your kind words, Alice."

"Of course, Catriona. I speak only the truth. Now, what else does a lady's maid do?" Alice asked, giggling. "Well, I shall tidy up here and then go down to the servant's quarters, introduce myself. And I do believe it's time for you to head down to breakfast with your family."

Catriona nodded.

A deep breath served her well as she walked down to the drawing room. Today, thankfully, the only people present would be the viscount and viscountess, and herself, of course. This was technically her manor now, but because she had no idea what she was doing, they were staying with her until she could cope on her own.

"A pleasure to see you this morning, Catriona," Bridget said as Catriona entered the room.

"Did you sleep well?" the viscount asked, looking at her and smiling over a cup of coffee. "And please, you can drop the formalities with me too, when it's just family. It's Anthony."

"Thank you, Anthony. I slept well, yes. And yourselves?"

"Very well, indeed," Bridget smiled.

Anthony only nodded in agreement with his wife. Catriona had come to learn over the course of the last few days that Anthony meant well, but he often remained silent when he wasn't sure what to say. Since he didn't know Catriona well, and she didn't know him either, there was always a bit of an awkward silence between them.

Catriona didn't mind. She was actually rather happy to know her cousin didn't try to fill the silences, but simply let them become comfortable in each other's company as time went on.

The silence didn't last long today, though. Thankfully, unlike Eleanor or Lady Spencer, Anthony never bothered her while she was eating breakfast.

"I have arranged an informal dinner later this evening," he announced, looking at Catriona. "I do hope you don't mind. I thought it might make for some rather more relaxed entertainment for you. I have invited my good friend Hamish over for dinner. You may have met him as Lord Milington a few days ago."

She didn't remember, but she smiled at the prospect.

"I would be pleased to see a friend of yours here at the manor," she said. "Currently, it is your home, too. Of course, you must continue to invite your friends whenever you wish."

"Then, it is settled," Anthony said. "Bridget, perhaps you could help Catriona pick out a dress for this evening? This might be her first proper dinner party."

"It will be, and so I would appreciate some help," Catriona admitted. "I've been rather . . . *overwhelmed* by things so far. It will make a nice change to relax and not have Lady Spencer critiquing my choice of dress for the evening."

Bridget and Anthony both let out a laugh.

"I think that would be horrible, indeed," Bridget finally said. "I'd be more than happy to help you pick out a suitable dress for the evening, especially since the modiste has not yet completed anything we have ordered for you. I'm sure I can find something nice to suit you. It's a good thing I already have an idea of what I shall wear."

Bridget threw a glance over at Anthony, but he was obliviously eating his breakfast. Catriona assumed that meant that Anthony had gifted his wife a new dress and the dinner party would be the first time she would wear it. *How sweet!*

Catriona was perfectly happy to borrow whatever gown Bridget thought best. After a lifetime of wearing grey dresses, having so much choice open to her now was difficult to cope with.

# Chapter Eight

That evening, Hamish arrived at Beaumont House for dinner. He admitted to himself that he was rather excited. Anthony's frequent invitations since Hamish's return to London made it almost feel like he had never been away. It was deeply gratifying. It also reminded him that his father didn't have control over *everything* he did. That was always a good reminder to have.

The butler escorted him into the drawing room, where he was met by Anthony.

"Oh, I'm so glad you could make it!" Anthony smiled widely at him. "I'm quite certain tonight is going to be wonderful, and you're going to be of tremendous help in getting Catriona ready to be presented to the *ton,* I'm sure of it."

"Well . . . as happy as I am to be here, I am honored to learn that you think I can be of help to Miss Beaumont at this early stage," Hamish said, adding in a lower voice, "I feel I must tell you, gossip is already circulating amongst the *ton* about her. Be careful."

Anthony let out a long sigh and scratched his head, frowning.

"It didn't take long for the news to spread . . . How in the world? We have been incredibly careful about who knows what. We've tried to make sure everyone knows she is to be presented this coming Season, but we've said nothing more about her."

Hamish nodded. "I was at a dinner with the Ashmores the other night. The ladies were gossiping about her, egged on by Lady Josette and her mother."

"Hamish, I don't know about you, but I feel sorry for any gentleman marrying into *that* family. They have such a reputation for gossip, and no one does anything because they're afraid they will be next. It is . . . so maddening to me." Anthony pursed his lips and frowned. "I pity the men who must marry Lady Josette and Lady Rosalie."

Hamish quickly glanced around the drawing room. No one else had entered yet, and he had a feeling it was because the ladies were upstairs getting ready, and other members of the Beaumont family had yet to arrive at the manor.

"Anthony, there is something I must confide in you now. My father . . . he wishes me to marry Lady Josette," Hamish said. "He believes the marriage will strengthen our business connections, but I think he's doing it to be sure I never have a chance at happiness, since he too was forced into a loveless marriage."

Anthony opened his mouth to respond, but at that moment, two ladies stepped into the room. One was, of course, the lovely Viscountess Beaumore—wearing a lovely lilac dress. The other was Miss Beaumont.

Miss Beaumont wore a pale blue dress with matching gloves, and Hamish swore his heart almost skip a beat when he realized just how far she had come from the poor looking young lady he had stumbled across on the stairs just a few days before. The pale blue complimented her eyes incredibly well, and she looked as though she had started to glow a little more since moving into the manor.

It wasn't but a moment later when he realized she was staring back at him. Perhaps she was still not entirely used to seeing well-dressed men in her vicinity. He was thankful when the butler announced the arrival of the dowager viscountess, Lady Spencer, her husband, and Mr. and Mrs. Mills.

If it had been anyone else in that group, the tender moment he had just shared—at least, he hoped it was a tender moment—with Miss Beaumont might have been considered scandalous. They had stared at each other for much longer than they should have, but it seemed Anthony and Bridget had been the only ones to catch it.

Thankfully, he knew Anthony would never say a thing about it. Bridget would talk to Miss Beaumont about it, most likely, and warn her to be careful of doing that again. Reputations were more important to ladies than to gentlemen. A lady could be utterly ruined before she had a chance to be presented . . . if the wrong things were told to the *ton*.

With the way the Ashmore family had been talking about Miss Beaumont at the tea party, Hamish quietly promised himself to do his best to give them absolutely nothing they could use against Miss Beaumont. If they wanted to gossip against her, they would have to find the reasons to do so themselves.

As he turned to continue a new conversation with Anthony, Hamish found himself being eyed by Lady Spencer. She turned her eyes away as soon as she was caught, but Hamish knew that look. It had been the same one he had seen her often give Bridget during the first few months of her courtship with Anthony.

Lady Spencer did not appear to approve of his presence there tonight. He wondered why not—his reputation was sound, and he did nothing to give the *ton* anything to gossip about.

But when he thought about it, he could understand Bridget having some reservations about him being around Miss Beaumont so much. His family's ties to the Ashmore family were well known, as was their reputation for ruining people by circulating rumors about people they sometimes didn't know at all. That was perhaps the one explanation he could *understand* for Lady Spencer being upset about him being there.

Other than that, he didn't know why she had felt the need to glare so hard at him.

Unless . . . was it possible she thought Hamish was an interloper and was only there to gather gossip about Miss Beaumont, to spread around the *ton*?

If Lady Spencer had been paying any kind of attention to how he presented himself and what he had left here in favor of a life in the Far East, she might have realized that he was not the one she needed to worry about in his family.

Hamish could easily see his father spreading rumors to the Ashmore family to besmirch Miss Beaumont's reputation in order to secure a marriage between Hamish and Lady Josette. *Thank God I didn't mention meeting Miss Beaumont to the old man . . .*

Bridget stepped forward a moment later, locking eyes with Anthony, then Hamish. It was as if she had something inside her that *sensed* when tension was brewing, as she clapped her hands loudly, and everyone looked at her.

Hamish quietly let out a sigh of relief. There was nothing he could have appreciated more, and it seemed Bridget had read his mind. That, or she had noticed how Lady Spencer had been staring at him. Hamish didn't care which. Whatever she was about to say, it was probably going to be enough to break the tension.

"Dinner is ready to be served," Bridget said. "Hamish, would you do the honor of kindly escorting Catriona to the dining hall tonight? We seem to have miscalculated when we invited everyone and left her without an escort."

Hamish only smiled at Bridget admiringly. That woman had a sense of how to frame things so they appeared to be entirely accidental. Whether this was one of those times, Hamish could only speculate. He had shared some thoughts with Anthony that could have very well informed the viscountess's decision to arrange the numbers so that Hamish *had* to escort Miss Beaumont.

It was unlikely, he thought, that Bridget would make such a mistake. *Still, it doesn't matter.*

Instead of dwelling on it, he turned to Miss Beaumont.

"Miss Beaumont, may I have the honor of escorting you to the dining hall?"

"I would be most honored, my lord," Miss Beaumont said, smiling shyly.

He offered her his arm. She linked arms with him, and they started towards the dining hall. As much as Hamish wanted to say something to her, he wasn't sure what would be appropriate just then. He could have talked about how exciting it was to be at a dinner party with her. Or that he was excited to see she was adjusting well to her status now she was a lady of wealth instead of living in an orphanage.

The problem with all those topics of conversation, however, was the knowledge that Lady Spencer was just a few feet behind them the entire time. He did not want to be overheard, so he decided to say nothing.

He was not to know that Lady Spencer had quite a reputation for wanting everything to happen *just so.* And if things didn't happen that way, she could have a bit of a fit. But she wouldn't scream or shout. Lady Spencer would simply glare at the offender, as if trying to convey through thought alone the horrors of their particular crime, growing even angrier at their failure to understand.

She had subjected Hamish and Miss Beaumont to that very same glare earlier in the evening.

If Lady Spencer had her way, he imagined he would never have been invited to the dinner because he would perhaps encourage Catriona to be as unladylike as possible, considering the way she had grown up. Of course, he didn't blame *that* on Miss Beaumont. To have grown up under such poor conditions as were found in an orphanage and then be thrust into the spotlight of wealth and class the next day, at such an age . . . He imagined he might well struggle with such a change in lifestyle too.

In the dining hall, Hamish pulled the assigned chair out for Miss Beaumont, three seats down from the viscount's place at the head of the table. Hamish was happy to find he had been placed directly opposite her. He was glad to see Bridget would be sitting to the other side of Miss Beaumont, while Anthony sat beside him.

"Thank you, Lord Milington."

Miss Beaumont offered him a smile as she sat down in the chair as elegantly as any duchess. He pushed the chair in for her, and for a moment, he thought her the picture of a true lady.

He sat down in his seat across the table from her, and dinner was soon served. As the dinner started, he was glad there was not much conversation around the table, and he and Miss Beaumont did not speak to each other. He struggled for a suitable topic. He was reluctant to mention living in the Far East; it was inevitable once people found out. And he wasn't even sure if Miss Beaumont knew or cared that he had been living so far away for the last few years.

Thankfully, no one seemed bothered with chatting; they were all far too concerned with their food, making sure to obey all the rules of etiquette. Miss Beaumont appeared to struggle slightly with some aspects of etiquette, but Hamish pretended not to notice. He had no reason to comment on anything she might do wrong, and he didn't want to be chastised by Lady Spencer.

He didn't want to subject Miss Beaumont to that, either.

As time went on, he couldn't help but notice that Lady Spencer had allowed her gaze to fall back on him. It was a deep, discerning glare. He still believed she was against his presence at the dinner, but the way Miss Beaumont had almost seemed to light up upon learning he was to be her escort to the dining hall made up for it.

Lady Spencer could keep her nose out of their business. Otherwise, she was only slightly better than the Ashmore family—as, at the very least, Lady Spencer knew when to keep her mouth shut about affairs she had no business gossiping about. The Ashmores had no such manners, to everyone's chagrin.

Once dinner was served, Hamish forced those thoughts away. This was no place to think of the Ashmore family, after all!

# Chapter Nine

Thrills spread down her arms and spine as Catriona linked arms with Hamish so he could escort through the house to the dining hall. Something about being near this man—Lord Milington when she actually addressed him in conversation, she quietly reminded herself— made her feel as though nothing else in the world mattered.

It took only a few moments to reach the dining hall, and she found herself rather surprised when he pulled the chair out for her.

"Thank you, Lord Milington," she said.

He nodded and smiled before pushing the chair in smoothly for her. After that, he went and found his seat across the table from her. However, as dinner was being served, she couldn't help but notice the way Lady Spencer was staring at Hamish. The glare was powerful and, Catriona thought, full of concern.

Puzzled, she turned away just as Hamish looked in her direction, to see that Lady Spencer had set her sights on her!

"Catriona, you ought to be presented to the *ton* within the next month," she declared. "It is obvious that there are people in the *ton* who will do whatever they can to spread *gossip*, and I for one believe you need to be ahead of that gossip. What better way to be ahead of it than to be presented formally to the *ton*?"

Catriona couldn't help but watch as Lady Spencer's eyes darted from her to Hamish at the word 'gossip' and then back again. From what she understood of Lord Milington's character, he would not gossip idly about her reputation. She didn't think she had much of one yet, anyway. The only thing people could potentially gossip over right then was the fact she had grown up in an orphanage.

She had made no secret of that. Why should she?

"Margaret," the dowager viscountess chimed in, "the Season is far from over. We could always delay her presentation until she is comfortable in her new role." She now looked to Catriona. "Gossip is something to be aware of, yes, but I do not believe those at this table would gossip idly with the intent to spread ill-rumors of you or your rise to your new status."

Catriona had been half paying attention to the conversation, but she did give Eleanor a nod. That much, she had figured. If Anthony felt comfortable inviting a friend to an informal family dinner with her being so new to the family, then Lord Milington must have a good reputation himself. Or Anthony knew him well enough to know he needn't worry about Lord Milington wanting to profit from idle gossip about a woman he hardly knew.

It was not hard, however, to see that he wanted to know her better. Catriona wondered if Lord Milington believed he was being subtle about it, or that she couldn't see it, but he was once more stealing glances at her from across the table. The thought filled her with a warm glow.

Now she had met him a few times, Catriona had concluded that Hamish was altogether a rather handsome man. He had lovely pale-blue eyes, with light-brown hair, which was swept out of his face and probably in need of a trim, and he was tall and broad-shouldered. It was that same figure which had attracted her attention that very first day, the one she had been admiring just before she tripped, and *he* had saved her . . . before she had learned she was the daughter of the late Viscount Beaumore. Now, taking secret glances at him herself across the table, she couldn't deny she liked the attention he paid her.

"I shall have to send word to Mr. Jones for dancing lessons, regardless," Lady Spencer said just then, clearly wishing to keep the conversation centered on Catriona's presentation to the *ton*. "He is the best teacher for someone so new to it, and I'm sure he could have you properly trained within the next month."

"Margaret, I hear he is fully booked for months ahead," Mrs. Mills said. "He's probably been asked to help lots of other young ladies, so they can also be presented to the *ton* this Season."

Lady Spencer grumbled something Catriona couldn't hear. So far, no one had cared to ask what she thought, though Eleanor had suggested waiting until Catriona felt more comfortable with the idea. In truth, she didn't know what she wanted. There was so much to learn. But she also knew that if she was not presented properly to the *ton*, it would be difficult to find a man to court her.

Since it had always been a dream of hers to marry, Catriona supposed that Lady Spencer had a point. Especially if she wanted to marry soon.

Before she could say anything, Anthony tapped on his glass. The rest of the table fell silent, and Catriona decided to hear what he had to say before she said anything about waiting or not.

"I propose we have a dancing lesson after pudding. Hannah, you're well-versed in playing the pianoforte, unless I'm mistaken, so would you be willing to provide the music for us tonight?"

Catriona didn't mind the idea too much. Perhaps having a start with people she was more comfortable with than a total stranger would help her learn.

"Oh, we could demonstrate a few steps of the waltz for Catriona, Anthony. I do so love the waltz." Bridget smiled widely.

Catriona thought it a wonderful idea. She'd always wanted to learn the waltz, such an airy, elegant dance. However, she knew there were those in High Society who considered it a dance fit only for engaged or married couples. Clearly, Lady Spencer wasn't one of them. However, she was determined not to show how excited she was by the idea.

So far, everything that had excited Catriona had been wrong in some manner in Lady Spencer's eyes. The morning when Alice had arrived stuck out in her mind as an example. She had gotten so excited about seeing her friend, all thought of propriety had gone right out of the window. Then again, she hadn't known the proper etiquette in that situation anyway.

She'd still gotten scolded by Lady Spencer, and the incident was continually brought up as an example of what not to do if she wanted to make sure that everyone spoke well of her instead of gossiping about her lack of manners.

It didn't take long for Catriona to be pulled out of her thoughts by a loud gasp. Everyone looked to its source, Lady Spencer. Catriona was not entirely surprised. It was *always* Lady Spencer, she was learning. Always. It didn't matter what the objection was, you could count on it to come from her.

Still, Catriona held her tongue to see what the objection was this time.

"The waltz is *far* too scandalous for Catriona to learn without a proper teacher in the room," Lady Spencer objected. "At least if Mr. Jones were teaching her, no one would have reason to speculate that she is learning so she might get married immediately after being presented to the *ton*. I will not have her learn the waltz so early!"

"Then, what do you suggest we do, Margaret?" Eleanor looked to her daughter.

"I suggest we focus on the country reels, instead. That at least she can do with men she has only just been introduced to or doesn't know well. There's no room for gossip there," Lady Spencer said. "I do believe she will have better luck with it, anyway. It doesn't require such detailed movements as the waltz, and it'll be easier for her to learn the waltz if she has other experience to build on."

"I think you have stumbled on a great idea, Anthony," Eleanor said. "We have no time to waste. Let us have a dancing lesson after pudding. But Margaret also has a good point. We can start her off with the country reels, and we shall have to save the waltz for when there is less chance of rumors starting."

Anthony nodded and sat down.

Catriona wondered why everyone was so concerned with rumors spreading over her sudden appearance as the late Viscount Beaumore's daughter. Would it really be the end of her time as a lady if she learned things out of order because she had to learn so much in such a short amount of time—and get it all right?

"What do you make of all of this, Catriona?" Lady Beaumore turned to her in a quiet moment as everyone else focused on eating their dinner.

"Is it so hard to ask what I want?" She furrowed her brows as she spoke. "I would love to learn the waltz, but no one has asked me what *I* make of being presented to the *ton*."

"Oh, Lady Spencer means nothing by it, I'm sure," Bridget said with a frown. "Isn't that right, Lady Spencer?"

The woman looked up from her dinner, and then squarely at Catriona.

"Someone who has grown up in an orphanage has no idea of the best way to learn everything necessary," Lady Spencer protested. "The waltz is one of the hardest dances to learn, and I do believe one must have *some* practice in other dances before you attempt to learn it." She turned to Catriona before asking, "Do you have a knowledge of the waltz? Or of the way one must move so that one appears utterly graceful and yet as if one is dancing on air, all without appearing to miss a single step?"

"N-n . . . no, Lady Spencer."

"That is exactly what I thought, Miss Beaumont," Lady Spencer said with an authoritative nod of her head. "The last thing we want is more than one rumor spreading through the *ton*, and that means you must learn things in a prescribed order, just as all the other ladies have."

Catriona sighed.

As she returned her attention to the food in front of her, she found Lord Milington stealing a glance at her. His eyes darted down to his food, and his cheeks flushed slightly. She couldn't help but smile a little. As difficult as it was to hear Lady Spencer tell her she did not know what was best for her own presentation to the *ton*, she was glad to see someone else was paying her some attention.

Lady Spencer started speaking to Lord Milington, claiming she could tell by his blush that he agreed with her idea and thanking him for understanding exactly how hard it had been for her ever since Catriona had come to claim her fortune. Catriona had no desire to listen to her, so, instead, she allowed herself to wonder what her life might have been like at this moment if she had grown up with these people.

She could almost guarantee she would have been asked to attend Anthony and Bridget's wedding. Lady Spencer probably wouldn't be as hard on her right now if Catriona had grown up a lady, as it fitted within her narrow standards. In other circumstances, the presentation ball the family was now working so hard to arrange would have been properly planned and executed, as Bridget's had no doubt been.

"Oh, what a lovely cake for pudding!"

Lord Milington's voice pulled her out of her thoughts.

One of the servants had brought in a beautiful sponge cake, layered with fruits and a drizzle of syrup. Catriona wondered what occasion called for such a beautiful cake, but after the thorough dressing down she had received from Lady Spencer, she was not in the mood to risk asking and receive another one.

"I thought tonight warranted a little something special," Anthony said. "To celebrate the addition of a wonderful new family member. Catriona, why don't you cut the cake?"

"Me? Are you sure, Anthony?" She looked at him and saw him nod. "All right, I will."

One of the servants passed her a knife, and she cut the cake gleefully. Then, Anthony took over, serving everyone a slice of cake, starting with Catriona. And it looked utterly delicious sitting in front of her.

"Go ahead," Anthony said. "Do not wait for us to finish serving, Catriona. Please. It is the *least* you deserve after how hard we have been on you."

This was accompanied by a harsh glance at Lady Spencer, whose cheeks did not flush in the slightest.

Catriona took a small bite of the cake. It was entirely too sweet for her to eat all of it just then, but it was very good. It had lemon icing and a cream filling.

She wished Alice could have shared her good fortune tonight, but as soon as dinner was finished, everyone gathered in the ballroom.

# Chapter Ten

Hamish stood in the ballroom of Beaumore Manor, watching Anthony and Bridget dance a country reel. They had decided to demonstrate for Catriona what it was supposed to look like. Both Anthony and Bridget had made it clear to Miss Beaumont before they started dancing, to the pianoforte played by Mrs. Mills, that they didn't expect her to be able to dance like that *tonight*.

He thought that was a good warning to give her.

However, he thought it was entirely unfair to Miss Beaumont that Lady Spencer had made such a fuss over the waltz. He didn't know if anyone else had been paying attention, but her eyes had started to sparkle at the thought of learning the dance. Sadly, since it was considered far too scandalous by Lady Spencer, they were going to skip it this time around.

He wondered if anyone would bother to ask Miss Beaumont what she wanted to learn. He had a feeling she wanted to dance the waltz. No matter its reputation for being a scandalous, romantic dance, Hamish liked it because it needed such composure to pull it off successfully. If Miss Beaumont could waltz while Lady Spencer had a fit over it, he had a feeling she would be able to hold her composure through anything.

Then again, that was simply something Hamish chose to believe.

When he glanced over at Miss Beaumont to see how she was faring while watching Anthony and Bridget dance the country reel, he couldn't help but feel sorry for her. Her eyes darted around, attempting to follow their every move and see if she could spot anything to make the dance easier to remember.

Unfortunately, she had truly been thrown into the deep end when it came to what was now expected of her. The *ton* could truly be a sink or swim matter, and he knew that one either would swim . . . or drown in its expectations.

It seemed as though Miss Beaumont was primed to drown if no one else in her family other than Anthony and Bridget took the time to explain to her what they were doing and why it was important. And how to do it. That was the most important thing.

Hamish wondered if Lady Spencer and the dowager viscountess had simply forgotten what it was like to be faced with all this as children and feeling overwhelmed by everything they were expected to memorize about being a lady before coming out. If that was the case, then of course it made sense that they were pushing to have Miss Beaumont learn everything she possibly could and be presented to the *ton* this Season.

Personally, Hamish didn't see why they couldn't wait a Season to do it and give her a full year to come to grips with everything she was supposed to learn.

However, in this moment, he wanted to help her prepare as best as he could. Watching her struggle to learn the country reel, even with Anthony offering his help as her partner, was tough. Eventually, Anthony and Bridget switched to the cotillion, which was not nearly as difficult, in his opinion, as the country reels could be.

He walked over to Miss Beaumont as Anthony helped Mrs. Mills find some proper music for the cotillion. She looked rather shocked to see him approaching her. He gave her a soft bow before daring to say anything—knowing that Lady Spencer was going to be criticizing everything Miss Beaumont did that night.

"May I have the honor of this next set, Miss Beaumont?" He smiled at her as he spoke.

Her cheeks flushed a deep crimson as she took his arm. He wondered if it was purely because she was not sure how she would fare out on the floor as his partner, or if it was because she was glad to be noticed by him. It didn't matter much to him.

"I'd be honored, Lord Milington."

He escorted her onto the dance floor. It didn't take long for him to get into position for the cotillion, and he felt tingles run up his spine as he placed a hand on her lower back to help guide her into the correct positions for the dance.

Mrs. Mills started the music, and Hamish found it easy enough to start dancing with Miss Beaumont. He'd grown up dancing to these songs. Of course, he would find it easy. However, despite his best lead, she still trampled his feet quite a few times as they worked their way around the ballroom, throwing off his pacing.

He understood. The cotillion could be difficult after trying the country reel, especially if she had been having problems keeping her feet in the right positions so that she wasn't trampling her partner's feet.

Hamish glanced around the room as he kept twirling her around the room. Everyone else had their eyes on them. Perhaps that was part of the reason why Miss Beaumont struggled to keep her eyes focused anywhere except on her feet.

As he pulled her closer for a turn at the end of one of the walks, Hamish leaned his head in close to hers.

"Pretend it's only the two of us in the ballroom and look up at me, Miss Beaumont. You might find your feet fly that way." He smiled at her. "It's all right to block out the rest of the surroundings but for your partner and the music when you are learning."

She nodded slowly.

Then, her eyes slowly came up to meet his. He felt her relax a little more into his grip. That was probably going to be another reason why she would be able to dance a little better come the end of the night, but he didn't want to start congratulating her just yet.

First, they had to finish the set he had asked her to dance with him.

It took several rounds of the cotillion to do that. Anthony and Bridget eventually joined them on the dance floor, and though Hamish could see how much fun the couple was having, simply enjoying a dance together. They only had to worry about not bumping into himself and Miss Beaumont. He couldn't help wishing Miss Beaumont could dance so easily for herself.

The rest of the rounds of the cotillion actually went quite smoothly. She only trampled his feet twice after he'd told her it was all right to pretend it was only the two of them in the ballroom. To help keep that feeling alive, he had only nodded or smiled when Anthony and Bridget passed them on the floor.

At the end of the music, Hamish pulled away softly from Miss Beaumont and offered his arm to her. He couldn't help but smile at her as she sheepishly put her hand on his arm. Slowly, they walked back to where everyone else waited for them. Anthony and Bridget didn't look any worse for wear for all the dancing they had done, and he imagined it was simply because they'd had plenty of practice, like himself.

In contrast, Miss Beaumont's face had turned a deep shade of crimson. She breathed heavily, as if she was not used to so much exercise in one activity.

However, as he escorted her back to where he'd found her, he couldn't help but feel disappointed that the dancing had finally come to an end. Of course, they were only practicing. At a real ball, how much more exciting it would be!

He hadn't thought he'd feel so disappointed about having to stop dancing with Miss Beaumont, though. No woman had ever made him feel like that before. Especially not Lady Josette.

"We'd best be on our way home, now the dancing is done for the night," Mrs. Mills said. "It was a pleasure to play the pianoforte for everyone. I hope we can do this again soon. It was fun. Anthony, thank you for such a wonderful suggestion."

"Yes, thank you, Anthony," Miss Beaumont echoed.

"You still have a long way to go, Catriona," Lady Spencer cautioned. "Do not celebrate just yet."

That made Miss Beaumont shrink away from Lady Spencer, but Bridget took her away before Lady Spencer could say anything more. Once everyone else had seen themselves out, Hamish turned to Anthony.

"Why don't you come join me for a game of billiards?" Anthony asked, smiling. "I think it's been far too long since we played."

"That would be grand."

The two men walked towards the billiards room.

Not long after they started playing, Anthony spoke up again.

"I appreciate you stepping up and helping Catriona with the dancing earlier this evening," he said. "Margaret appears to have it in for her, but I can't imagine why. Perhaps it's simply because she cannot fathom someone who doesn't know what they're doing being part of this family. She was the same with Bridget."

"I remember how she treated Bridget. Besides, that's what friends are for," Hamish said with a smile. "I would be lying if I didn't say it was a pleasure to dance with Miss Beaumont, despite her lack of experience. She learns quickly. I don't think Lady Spencer has any real reason to worry about the presentation."

"Neither do I, but I cannot stop her from criticizing everything Catriona does," Anthony said, shaking his head. "I do think it would be a good idea for Catriona to get out of the house for a bit, though. Margaret insists that she stay in the manor until we get a chance to present her to the *ton.* But I can see how much she wants to go out and see some of the places she perhaps hasn't been able to visit before."

"Were you thinking of anything in particular?" Hamish asked.

"Richmond Park. I was thinking of taking the family there for a picnic in three days' time."

Anthony hit his cue against the balls, and Hamish silently watched them scatter.

"Perhaps you'd like to join us?" Anthony said as he repositioned for another shot.

"You, your family, and Richmond Park?" Hamish smiled. "It sounds like a good place to be. I'll happily come along. Besides, I think Miss Beaumont could use another friendly face if she's going to be out in a sea of people who are just waiting to judge everything little thing she does—whether she knows it or not."

"You've got that right."

Anthony sighed.

"Now, the other reason I invited you to play billiards . . . you said you want us to go into business together. But with the news of Catriona taking over everything of her father's, we haven't had a chance to properly discuss what sort of venture exactly," he continued. "I hope you don't mind talking over it while we play billiards."

"I'd be honored to talk business *and* play billiards with you," Hamish joked.

Anthony shook his head.

They had a very good relationship, if Hamish had to say anything about it. The fact that Anthony had gone out of his way to find time for them to talk business was part of the reason he felt Anthony was a good friend to have.

They continued their game as they discussed what kind of trades they were interested in and how they wanted to proceed. If things panned out properly, Hamish had a feeling he wouldn't have to entirely rely on his father's . . . *antiquated* view of marriage.

After all, he wanted to marry for love. He knew it was out there somewhere. Anthony and Bridget had taught him that much, no matter what his father had tried to instill in him, that love didn't exist.

And Hamish simply couldn't abide the idea of marrying someone like Lady Josette Ashmore when Miss Catriona Beaumont was staring him right in the face.

# Chapter Eleven

The next morning, Hamish muttered to himself as he got up. He hadn't had too much drink; a hangover was actually the least of his problems. One might have actually solved the next problem, in his opinion. He was meant to meet with his father and Lord Isaac Ashmore, the Earl of Ashington. It was never something he was going to look forward to or enjoy, and he could have done with a good excuse to cry off.

Regardless, he arrived at Ashington Manor for the meeting without any problems. He'd rather be on time and at least keep his father off his back than not attend and make his father angry with him. He didn't want to deal with that today.

The butler escorted him to the office, where the earl was pouring drinks for the three of them.

"Ah, right on time," his father said. "I'm glad you could join us, Hamish. I was starting to worry you might have had too much fun last night and had neglected to get up on time."

"I simply got a little behind this morning is all, Father," Hamish said. "A pleasure, Lord Ashington, to see you this morning."

"And you as well, Lord Milington. I'm pleased to see you are punctual."

With that, Hamish sat down and took the glass offered to him. The earl took a seat behind his large desk. Hamish knew that the man would soon start bragging about his business prowess, as was his habit in company. It didn't take long for Lord Ashington to start boasting about the vast profits he was raking in from his shares in the tea and coffee trades.

Hamish had never understood why anyone would choose to do business with the odious man, who simply wanted money and didn't care how he made it. Far better to go into business with a reputable man like Anthony.

He swore that, sometimes, he didn't understand what his father was thinking when it came to the kind of business deals they made.

"We would all benefit, of course, from an arranged marriage between Hamish and Josette," the earl had said at one point. "With my shares in the tea and coffee trade, and your business savvy, Eldridge, I do believe we would have a perfect way to increase profits all round and ensure our legacies."

Hamish gulped hard.

Even though he knew that was what was expected of him, he couldn't imagine sharing the rest of his life with the insufferable Lady Josette.

As he attempted to picture what his life would be like married to that woman, he found all he could picture instead was an image of Miss Beaumont's smiling face. He wanted nothing more than to make her life better, *easier.* And though he couldn't be entirely sure yet, Hamish could have sworn that something was starting to stir in his chest every time he thought of her.

"Hamish, do you have any questions for the earl about his business?"

His father's voice snapped him out of the daze that thinking about Miss Beaumont had put him into. He couldn't believe he had allowed himself to start thinking about her like that . . . but honestly, when the choice came down to Lady Josette or anyone else . . . Hamish would have taken any other lady in marriage over one of the Ashmore sisters. If they could be considered ladies, knowing how many lives they had ruined with their idle gossip.

For show, Hamish asked Lord Ashington a few general questions about his business. However, the answers were vague, the man's tone suggesting there was something about the questioning which made him uncomfortable.

Why should the earl be uneasy, unless he was hiding something about the way he conducted business?

"If you are so worried about my affairs," the earl eventually said, clearly frustrated with Hamish for questioning his intentions, "I could arrange for my man of business to provide you with the necessary accounts."

"It would be wonderful if you could arrange it," Hamish returned coldly. "I would greatly appreciate it."

The earl poured them one more drink to celebrate. Hamish drank it out of civility. He couldn't imagine why the earl had been so uneasy with his questions about his business practices. Surely, if one intended to invest in a business, then it only made sense to ask what were really very general questions. Hamish hadn't even touched on any specifics. He'd mainly asked about how they made their money, how much they made and spent, stuff of that sort.

With the drinks finished, the earl dismissed them—first thanking them for taking the time to discuss things with him. Hamish nodded a stern goodbye. His father seemed pleased and smiled at the earl before they left.

They had only just reached the hallway, with Hamish doing his best not to engage in conversation with his father, when they were met by Lady Henriette, Lady Josette, and Lady Rosalie.

"Oh, Lord Milington, Your Grace," Lady Henriette said. "What a pleasure it is to see you both today."

"And you, of course, Lady Henriette," his father said with a bow.

Hamish bowed as well, but he kept his eyes on the floor, hoping to deter Lady Josette from attempting anything.

As soon as he made the mistake of looking up, however, he found Lady Josette was ready for him, fluttering her eyelashes at him.

"Good morning, Lord Milington. How lovely to see you," she said.

"A pleasure, Lady Josette."

Hamish wanted to *run*. The fact that she could be so sweet when she wished to, to suit her purpose, made him even surer he didn't want to marry her. If anyone upset her, he had no doubt she would retaliate viciously, spreading ruinous gossip about them. One might escape the worst of it in public, but in private . . . The thought made him shudder.

The ladies didn't stay for long, for which Hamish was quietly thankful. He assumed they had engineered the 'chance' meeting, to remind him he was supposed to be marrying Lady Josette. But the image of Miss Beaumont's smiling face still remained in his head, and he used it to carry him through the evening until he could leave.

If it were up to him and not Society, he would not have anything to do with the Ashmore family.

He reached his carriage and was just getting into it when his father clearing his throat behind him made him stop. Hamish squared his shoulders and turned.

"Yes, Father?"

This was one of those moments when Hamish honestly wished for the days when he was in the Far East and his father could only try to control him through his letters. Stern, cold letters, talking about nothing but business. After a while, he'd simply ignored them, and there had been nothing the old man could do about it. Now, with all the pressure his father was putting on him to force him to marry Lady Josette, he wished him far away.

"Can we meet for drinks at my club to discuss matters?"

Hamish nodded. At least he wasn't expected to go home. Going to the club would mean his father wouldn't make a scene. Though he imagined his father was thinking the same thing about him and his 'ways,' hence his choice of venue.

It didn't matter. The carriage took him to his father's club, and he and the old man were eventually seated at a secluded table in one of the lounge bars.

His father looked at him with a stern expression before speaking.

"We ought not stall on our arrangement with the Earl of Ashington," his father finally said. "This is a good for both our families. Why do you insist on holding back? Lady Josette is a lovely young lady, and I can guarantee you won't find a woman of more grace and refinement in London than her and her sisters, Hamish."

It took everything in Hamish not to laugh. He turned it into a cough at the last moment, hoping his father had not caught on to just how absurd he believed that statement was in describing Lady Josette and her character.

"I wish to have something more to my marriage than simply your convenience, Father," he finally said after regaining his composure. "Yes, she is quite a lovely woman to look at, but . . . I cannot see anything more than that. She'd be a great woman to marry for business. But I do not want to marry. Not for business, at least."

His father chuckled.

Why had he expected his father to understand that there was more to marriage than making money?

"Hamish, I don't know what more you could possibly want in a wife," his father said. "Besides, you would be a fool to marry for love. No such thing exists."

"Father, surely you cannot truly believe that when one can see happy couples around London all the time."

Hamish knew this was turning into a desperate attempt to keep his father from agreeing to marry him off to someone he could not stand, but he had to try. Lady Josette was the kind of woman he could imagine his father marrying if he was young. But Hamish was not his father, and he didn't share the sensibilities that would allow him to marry Lady Josette for the reasons his father gave.

"My marriage to your mother was not one of love, if I must remind you," his father said. "As for the other couples, of course, one can marry for this . . . *love* you're so fond of . . . when one is not worried about a reputation.

The lower classes of London have the fantasy that they can marry whoever they want so long as they are able to stand the sight of them. We have not that fantasy but have the luxury of marrying to better our positions and allowing our children to enjoy what we have. Can you not see that I am thinking of your sons and daughters?"

As much as Hamish wanted to argue that even within the *ton*, one shouldn't have to marry solely out of practicality. Love wasn't just for the lower classes. But he knew his father was far too pragmatic to see it. If he could live happily with a marriage of convenience, then Hamish supposed there was no hope for his father ever seeing the argument for a marriage based on love. But Anthony and Bridget, as a High Society love match, proved his point.

"I refuse to have this argument with you, Father," Hamish eventually said. "We have our own very different beliefs when it comes to marriage, and we will never agree. But I can tell you this much: growing up watching you and Mother together is the reason I refuse to marry in the same manner. If there is merit to a business arrangement and I like the woman's personality, perhaps. But you could never convince me to marry Lady Josette for that alone."

He refused to make the argument against Lady Josette based on her personality either, as again, this was a woman he was almost positive his father would want to marry if he were young enough. Considering how much his father wanted to push him into a marriage that would trap him with someone like his father for the rest of his life, he didn't have to go very far to make that leap.

He got up from the table and walked away from his father.

The last thing he wanted was to marry to impress his father or to simply marry at the proper age, according to what Society deemed right.

As he walked away, he couldn't help but wonder what in the world Miss Beaumont planned to do when she was faced with the prospect of marriage. She would be presented to the *ton* and almost immediately beset upon by suitors . . . all looking for her money because she wouldn't know any better . . .

# Chapter Twelve

Three days after her dancing lesson under Anthony's instruction, Catriona couldn't help but feel quite excited. She was finally being allowed out of the manor for something other than walking around the grounds with Alice or one of the other ladies of the house. Anthony had decided it was time to attend a picnic at Richmond Park, and she was glad everyone agreed she deserved some time to simply relax without worrying about her presentation to the *ton*.

As Alice walked into the bedchamber, Catriona followed her and went straight to her wardrobe. Two new dresses from the modiste had finally arrived the day before, and she was delighted with them. Both were beautiful morning dresses, high-waisted, one a sprigged pale-blue and the other a beautiful pale-lilac muslin, with matching silk ribbons.

"They're both lovely, aren't they, Alice?" She turned to Alice, holding up the dresses.

"They are, but that flush on your cheeks says something more. You look flustered."

Catriona looked up at Alice's face, somewhat surprised. Her friend looked concerned, her expression one which Catriona had seen many times before. In truth, Alice had hit the nail on the head. She had somehow divined that part of Catriona wanted to look her best for Hamish, Lord Milington . . . or whatever his proper address was supposed to be. That was what was making her cheeks flush—deciding what to wear when she never knew if she might bump into him.

When Anthony had mentioned inviting his friend Hamish to join them at Richmond Park, Catriona's heart leaped, but then she started to fret. All her thoughts suddenly turned to the problem of choosing the right dress to wear for the occasion. It was not out of vanity but out a desire to feel confident in her own appearance, which she hoped would give her a confident attitude when conversing with him. At least, that was what she told herself as she tried to untangle her feelings at the prospect of seeing him again.

All that passed through Catriona's mind in seconds before she turned to Alice and said, "Nothing's wrong." Then, she let out a sigh.

"Well, I simply have no idea which dress to wear. They're both so beautiful. You know I've never had such beautiful clothing before . . . and I don't know which is more suitable for the park. And what if I get it get dirty? Laundering dresses like these is far different to washing our old gray ones at the orphanage."

Alice laughed. "I honestly don't think you have to worry about laundering things anymore, Catriona. Somebody gets paid to do that," she said.

There was a knock at the door before anything more could be said.

"Come in," Catriona called, laying the two dresses on her bed as the door opened behind her.

"What's all the fuss about? I was coming to see if you needed help . . . and I heard conversation going on," Bridget said as she entered the room.

"I can't decide which dress to wear to the park today, Bridget," Catriona told her, gesturing at the gowns on the bed. "They are so fine, what if I was to get them dirty at the park?"

"Oh, never mind that, Catriona," Bridget said, chuckling. "In the unlikely event that it gets dirty, it will be cleaned. That is not your concern. However, I believe the pale-blue dress would be becoming today. It matches your eyes. That was the reason I gave you the pale-blue gown for the dinner the other night, after all," Bridget said, smiling at her.

Catriona cast a glance over the dresses again. She had to admit Bridget was right. Perhaps it was admiration for her appearance in the pale-blue gown that had caused Hamish to stop speaking so suddenly the other night. It was a pleasant thought. Pale blue it was!

"Well, then, I shall trust your judgement today," Catriona said. "Alice, will you help me put on the blue dress, then?"

Alice nodded.

"I shall go and get ready myself," Bridget said. "When you're ready, why don't you meet us in the main hall?"

"All right, thank you, Bridget," Catriona said as Bridget left the room. As soon as the door closed behind her, Alice looked at her friend searchingly.

"I think I know why you were so flustered earlier," Alice said as she helped Catriona step into the dress so they could fit the bodice properly, "you were in a panic because the viscount has invited Lord Milington to the picnic—and you didn't know which dress would make the best impression on him!"

"Do I have to answer, Alice?"

Alice laughed a little as she pulled the bodice closed around Catriona's chest and began to tighten the laces.

"No, it's obvious. This morning gown is gorgeous. I'm a little jealous, Catriona. I suppose you have a hat to go with it?"

"The hat boxes are at the top of the wardrobe, it's in there somewhere."

When the dress was on, she looked at herself in the looking glass, turning this way and that, hardly able to believe it was her. The gown made her look . . . beautiful. The blue perfectly set off her eyes, just as Bridget had said. The dress flowed down her body flatteringly as she smoothed it. Her excitement rose. What would Lord Milington think of her in it?

Alice eventually found the matching hat and styled Catriona's hair around it, with curls at the front to frame her face.

"You look wonderful," she told Catriona, handing her a pair of white gloves to wear, then helping her put her shoes on. "There, I think you're ready."

"I just need my reticule," Catriona got up and fetched it from the nightstand.

"You look the picture of a viscount's daughter, Catriona," Alice said, grinning. "To the manor born. To think I'm a part of all this now because we were friends at the orphanage." She let out a soft laugh.

As she looked at herself in the looking glass, Catriona couldn't help but laugh too. Thank goodness Alice had been willing to come and work as her lady's maid. Having her at the manor was helping Catriona enormously. She could always be her true self with Alice. Only Alice could truly understand what a large adjustment this new life called for Catriona to make.

Catriona and Alice left the room and headed for the stairs.

"I can hardly believe how you managed to rescue me from the orphanage, too," Alice said. "I owe you for that, Catriona. I don't know how I can ever repay you, but I swear I will somehow."

"Alice, you owe me nothing. It's me who owes you," Catriona confessed. "You are my best friend, and just as you made our time in the orphanage better, you are helping me now just by being here and understanding my struggles. I can't thank you enough for being my friend and coming here."

Alice smiled and nodded. "Thank you," she said, as they arrived at the head of the stairs and saw the others waiting below.

As she and Alice descended, Catriona couldn't help noticing how Bridget and Anthony were staring at her. It was as if they were almost expecting her to suddenly topple over. She smiled to herself; she had become a lot better and walking up and down the manor stairs elegantly, as any lady should.

It helped her now to be wearing an elegant dress. She felt much more at ease going down the stairs knowing she needn't worry about watching her every step. It also helped that there were no distractions, such as having handsome Lord Milington to look at as he passed her by on the stairs.

"You look beautiful in that dress, Catriona, just as I thought you would," Bridget said. "You and I will be sharing a carriage with Anthony. Your maid will go in the other carriage with the other servants."

She looked at Alice as she spoke, who bobbed a curtsey and nodded. She looked down meekly as she followed them out to the waiting carriages with Bridget's lady's maid.

Catriona watched as a footman opened the door to the carriage. Anthony helped her into the carriage first, and then Bridget. She didn't mind so much the order, and she supposed there was a reason behind it. There was always a reason behind the way things were done in a family like hers.

Anthony was the last into the carriage, the footman shutting the door behind him before taking up his position at the back.

"You're going to love Richmond Park, Catriona. It's simply beautiful," Bridget said as the carriage started off. "It's full of nature and picturesque scenes. You might even see the deer. And there are plenty of other sights to see and things to do."

"It sounds lovely," Catriona said, trying to keep her excitement under control.

"My favorite parts are the walks around the different ponds and the lake, especially on a warm day like this," Anthony pitched in. "You have to be careful not to slip on the mud if it has rained recently, but the ponds are worth seeing."

"We might even see some swans," Bridget added.

While they continued to talk, Catriona hoped to be able to relax at the park. The rest of the family was going to be there, and she knew some of them weren't keen on her being out in public until she had been presented to the *ton*. Lady Spencer was among them.

Her opinion, as far as Catriona could gather, was that the *ton* would have less to gossip about—for better or worse—the less she was seen before her presentation. While she appreciated Lady Spencer looking out for the reputation that she now had to protect with her life, Catriona still wished she might be a little less bossy about it.

Even Eleanor seemed to give into her demands at times, and no one bothered to ask what Catriona herself wanted half the time. That was really what bothered her about how they were all handling her arrival into the family.

Thankfully, the spotlight was off her today. The picnic was a way to simply get away from the manor for a few hours, and Anthony had invited the rest of the family so that Catriona wouldn't feel so alone in the crowd.

While she appreciated his thoughtfulness, she wasn't sure things would work out exactly as Anthony intended.

Eventually, the carriage pulled into the park. Anthony helped both herself and Bridget alight, and Catriona looked around her. From what she could see, the park was absolutely gorgeous. Other people and families were out too, but that was all right. She didn't mind getting lost among so many other people.

To be one in a crowd was actually comforting to Catriona.

She then noticed two other carriages pulling up beside theirs. One carried Alice and two other servants. The other . . . she couldn't stop her heart from thudding in her chest when she saw Lord Milington alighting from the other carriage.

She'd sincerely hoped he would have arrived before them so she wouldn't have to get nervous about it. But now she had seen him, that no longer mattered. Seeing Lord Milington in such an open environment, where the *ton* could draw any conclusion it wished, could leave her a target of gossip, according to Lady Spencer. But Catriona did not care what the *ton* might think of her yearning to be around Lord Milington.

She was simply glad that *someone* Anthony had invited didn't entirely care about such things either.

# Chapter Thirteen

Hamish almost stumbled back against his carriage when he lost his breath upon locking eyes with Miss Beaumont. Her hair had been pinned back to frame her face beautifully beneath her pretty hat, which was adorned with blue ribbons to match her eyes and white rose buds to complement her complexion. He thought she looked striking.

Similarly striking was the dress she had chosen for the day, a pale-blue morning dress, and the color lit up her remarkably blue eyes. She had certainly transformed from the young woman he had prevented from falling on her face on the manor stairs so many days ago. If he hadn't been able to see her transformation over the days, he would have sworn this was an entirely different woman!

Taking a deep breath, he walked over to her, removed his hat, and bowed. But somehow, she managed to make it difficult for him to breathe at all, and he struggled to compose himself.

"Good morning, Miss Beaumont," he said.

"Good morning, Lord Milington," Miss Beaumont replied, smiling, her eyes shining as she dipped into an elegant curtsey.

Hamish was impressed. Her family had been working hard on instilling perfect decorum into her, and he could tell the hard work was paying off.

As she came up from the curtsey, he watched her to make sure she didn't wobble. That's what he told himself, anyway, knowing deep down that it was merely a good excuse to look at her because she was beautiful.

"The picnic is over by the Pen Ponds, Hamish," Anthony said as they headed into the park. "The servants should have it all set up by now."

"A picnic near Pen Ponds sounds delightful, Anthony," Hamish said, gravitating to Miss Beaumont's side.

The rest of the Beaumonts soon joined them, and Hamish kept a close eye on those who had earlier complained about the way Miss Beaumont dressed and acted. However, it appeared that everyone, even Lady Spencer, was quite pleased with her today. Her appearance was entirely in line with that of a proper lady. "Well, Catriona, "you look every inch the perfect lady today,"

Lady Spencer said.

"Thank you, Lady Spencer," Catriona replied with a gracious nod.

Hamish sensed that Miss Beaumont had been waiting to hear something like that from her aunt, as she smiled.

"Perhaps there is hope after all," Lady Spencer put in.

But she left it at that. Hamish could tell she was trying her best to be helpful, but sometimes, her criticisms were hurtful to Miss Beaumont, he could tell. He wondered if someone had tried to tell Lady Spencer so, and then he remembered that Lady Spencer seldom listened to anyone.

And she was unlikely to stop if she saw it as necessary to get the results she wanted and protect the Beaumont family name.

"Well, now we are all gathered," Anthony said with a smile, "I do believe we might make our way to the picnic."

Hamish looked back at Miss Beaumont, locking eyes with her for just a moment and seeing a flash of something there. He decided to act on it.

"May I have the honor of escorting you, Miss Beaumont?" He smiled as he held his arm out to her.

"Of course, you may, Lord Milington," Miss Beaumont replied, also smiling.

She took his arm, and they started to follow after the rest of the family. Hamish walked quietly with her for a few moments. The park was huge, and it would take several minutes at least to get to the pond for their picnic.

"I know we've been seeing each other quite a bit recently, but I feel as though I barely know anything about you other than how new you are to High Society, Miss Beaumont," Hamish started. "What are some of your interests? I mean, the things you liked doing before finding out about . . . all of this?" He gestured with his eyes at the family walking ahead of them.

Miss Beaumont gave him a startled look before pursing her lips. She remained silent a moment or two, clearly thinking, before saying, "I love to read."

He noticed that, as she spoke, something took over her face and she appeared quite animated. He realized she was excited at being asked about herself and was keen to share her love of reading with someone who had finally shown an interest.

Hamish smiled. He believed everyone should have a hobby they were passionate about, and reading was certainly something he approved of and enjoyed.

"And what are some of your favorites? I'm always looking for new books to read," he said.

"Well, I can't recommend many, I'm afraid. You see, I haven't had much time to read lately. At the orphanage, we had very few books, and they were old and not in good condition. Not many of the children could read, but we older ones, if they thought us clever enough, were taught, in case we could find work as a clerk or something of that ilk. So, there was a small library there, and I enjoyed Robinson Crusoe and some of the travel books, when I wasn't working, that is," Miss Beaumont told him, her face shining up at him. "And since moving to . . . well, you know, I have begun reading Miss Austen. She is marvelous."

"I am glad, but it sounds as though you didn't have as much time to read at the orphanage as you would have liked . . . if you had to work too," Hamish said with the frown."

"Yes, you're right. We weren't allowed much free time," she replied, her smile fading a little. Something akin to a look of remembrance passed over her face, and he noticed she quickly did her best to conceal it by fussing with the ribbons on her hat.

"Were you treated well at the orphanage?"

Hamish couldn't explain why he suddenly wanted to know, other than something in his heart tugged at him on seeing her enthusiasm fade.

"Well . . . it depends on how you look at it, I suppose," she said. "Younger children have it easier than the older ones."

Hamish raised an eyebrow. What on earth did she mean by that?

"In what way?" he asked.

"Well, the younger you are, the greater the chance of getting adopted, which is what the orphanage wants," Miss Beaumont explained. "And, well . . . the older you get, the less likely you are to be adopted, so you become just another mouth to feed. If you don't work around the orphanage, there's a certain age when you can't stay there any longer. You're expected to leave and find a job."

"And were you close to that age before you were brought to Beaumore Manor?"

She nodded. "In fact, I should have left two years ago, but I worked hard in the kitchens, you see. But it's because the orphanage puts a lot of time and resources into the younger children. They're the ones who get the good food, new clothing . . ."

"What do you mean, they put their resources into the younger children?"

Hamish couldn't ignore the way his stomach started to turn while she was speaking. Was it possible she was going to reveal that she had been mistreated? The thought made anger flare inside him. If that was the case, it would be his personal crusade to have the place inspected and shut down if necessary.

"The older children aren't treated very well. I-I . . . well, let us just say that it is not something I would speak of willingly to many others," she admitted.

His entire body tensed at the admission. If what she said was true, and he had no reason to doubt it, then, for some time before she had been brought to Beaumore Manor, she must have been working hard to keep her place at the orphanage. What a desperate situation!

"Oh . . . I'm very sorry to hear that, Miss Beaumont."

He didn't really know how to respond. How did one respond when they learned that someone had spent many years suffering because they were considered too old to be adopted?

"As I said, I worked in the kitchens, helping the cook prepare the meals," Miss Beaumont continued. "At first, the work was difficult. But the more I did it, the less it became work, and the more I loved cooking. When I first arrived at Beaumore Manor, I'll admit, I thought the reason I had been brought there was because I was going to be taking the place of one of the servants who had left suddenly. I never in my wildest dreams imagined I would be the *daughter* of the late viscount."

Hamish pursed his lips.

"I'm so sorry to hear that, Miss Beaumont. Well, you can be assured that you need not ever be mistreated like that again."

"I am well aware of that, Lord Milington," Miss Beaumont said as she turned to face him. "That is why I make sure to treat all the servants at the manor with respect. It's actually led to more than one disagreement between me and Lady Spencer. The work of a servant is not that of a lady, she says. It matters not what I know of how hard they have to work. I am not allowed help them."

Hamish laughed.

"Lady Spencer is certainly a lady with opinions, but I suppose she means well, Miss Beaumont," he said. "A lady's reputation in the *ton* is everything. Especially when your background is so unusual and likely to stir up rumors because you did not grow up in the same elevated circle as them. Everyone will be curious to know why you grew up in an orphanage and why it took so long for the *ton* to know of your existence."

It was at that point that they drew near to the picnic site. The servants had done a beautiful job of setting everything up. He noticed how Miss Beaumont exchanged a meaningful glance with one particular servant, a young maid who looked to be about the same age as her, before she resumed speaking.

"No one will believe that I have not the slightest idea why," she told him.

Miss Beaumont laughed, and Hamish had to admit it was good to see she had a sense of humor about the situation. In fact, despite the way his heart had squeezed painfully when she had revealed she had been treated terribly after not being adopted, he was glad to find she was not one of those ladies who would only talk about the weather or the pianoforte with him.

Some ladies thought it was best way to keep conversation light and keep a man from believing there was more to them than met the eye, but Hamish whole-heartedly disagreed with that policy. He wanted to hear their opinions on everything.

However, before they could talk more, they arrived at the picnic site, where some large blankets had been set out for them to sit upon beneath some trees.

"Well, I do believe we are here," she said. "Thank you for the escort, Lord Milington."

"Of course. Thank you for allowing me the honor," he said as she pulled away from his arm.

As Miss Beaumont sat down with the other ladies and settled her skirts elegantly about her, Hamish went over to sit with Anthony, regretting having to leave her. But as much as he wanted to continue their discussion, he knew that under the watchful eye of Lady Spencer, it was a bad idea to try his luck.

## Chapter Fourteen

As Catriona sat down on the blanket, she couldn't *believe* she had just revealed so much to Lord Milington about growing up in the orphanage. The last thing she wanted was his pity. He was such an honorable young man, she didn't know how to cope with the thought of him pitying her. It was such a horrid thought, she didn't dare dwell on it.

"I have some good news, everyone."

And, for once, Catriona was glad to hear Lady Spencer interrupt her thoughts—even though she knew it was likely going to have something to do with the way she was being prepared for her presentation to the *ton*.

"Mr. Jones has finished with his dancing commitments far earlier than we originally expected," she continued. "That means he will be able to spend more time teaching you, Catriona."

Catriona managed a smile. She would rather continue to learn the dances with Lord Milington at her side, but she knew Lady Spencer would *never* allow that since they were not officially courting. Then again, what would she say if she knew how much Catriona wanted to court him despite Lady Spencer suspicions of him being the outsider spreading the rumors about her?

"Thank you for taking the effort to arrange that for me," Catriona said politely.

Lady Spencer smiled, satisfied. Catriona wished that, just for once, she would be consulted on what it was she wanted to do in order to learn the necessary dances . Her aunt seemed oblivious to that, though. So, for now, Catriona had to do things her way.

"Of course, Catriona. Your presentation to the *ton must* be a success, and Mr. Jones is the *only* teacher I trust to teach you how to dance in such a short time," Lady Spencer added pointedly, frowning as Lord Milington came over and sat near to Catriona.

Catriona wanted to run from the picnic then. She knew Lady Spencer disliked Lord Milington being there. Was it because she thought he should be minding his own affairs instead of being included in the family's plan to make sure Catriona was successfully presented to Society?

In the meantime, the two maids had been spreading out the refreshments for the picnic. Catriona was thankful for the distraction. She'd had quite enough of her aunt attempting to keep a tight hold on everything she did. She wished someone would ask her what she wanted for her new life.

After the refreshments had been properly laid out, Lord Milington smiled softly at her from across the blanket.

"Miss Beaumont, I have been thinking about what you said about your love of reading. May I suggest you join a circulating library when you get the chance?" he said. "I do believe you would find they have plenty of new books to keep you occupied."

"Thank you for the suggestion, your lordship, but I fear it will be some time before I have that leisure," she said. "As you know, my family are intent on getting me ready for my coming out. There is a lot to learn about being a lady in a very short time."

"You'll do just fine, Miss Beaumont. You've got some of the best helping you to prepare."

Butterflies fluttered in her stomach as he spoke, and she sincerely wished there wasn't so much ceremony involved in being able to court someone. All she wanted, more than anything in the world, was to ask Lord Milington if they would be able to start courting soon. However, Catriona knew that more than one person in attendance would disapprove.

Lady Spencer was only one of them. Although she suspected that Anthony and his friend, in particular, would like to hear her thoughts on the matter, she didn't believe anyone else would agree. It seemed as if she would have to stick to the rules of High Society for the time being. She would have to wait for Lord Milington to initiate any developments between them.

And she hated the thought. Part of her believed it was only a matter of time before he acted, but another part wasn't even sure he saw anything in her to make him wish to do so.

"Would you two like to join me and Bridget in a walk to Pen Ponds?"

Anthony's voice broke in on her reverie.

"Yes, that would be lovely."

"Yes, indeed, thank you, Anthony."

They spoke in unison, and Catriona felt her cheeks grow hot. As she stood up, Catriona noticed Lady Spencer giving her a cold stare, but she was distracted when Lord Milington rose too.

He extended his hand towards her.

"Here, let me help."

She placed her hand in his, and tingles ran up her spine. Once again, she was touched by his thoughtfulness. How could Lady Spencer believe he was here to spread rumors instead of supporting a friend through a troubling change?

It didn't take long before she, Anthony, Bridget, and Lord Milington were walking together down one of the paths towards Pen Ponds. They made light conversation, and the atmosphere grew more relaxed, Catriona noticed, now they were away from Lady Spencer. Happy to be on Lord Milington's arm, she took the opportunity to look around the park.

Pen Ponds was simply glorious, and Catriona was charmed to see there were plenty of swans in the water.

"Why don't we feed the swans? They'll surely love it," Anthony said as Catriona caught her breath at the lovely scene.

Everyone took a piece of bread from the bag Anthony had brought. Catriona tore off small pieces and tossed them to the swans, who gathered eagerly to eat it, much to her delight.

Just then, she saw three ladies approaching them.

"Oh dear . . . it's the Ashmores."

Bridget had appeared behind them and was whispering to Anthony. Since Catriona stood just behind them, she could hear every word. Who were the Ashmores? Why should the others be worried about their approach?

Catriona straightened up from feeding the swans. She wasn't sure what to expect, but she could see how uncomfortable Anthony, Bridget, and especially Lord Milington now looked as the three ladies drew level with them.

The eldest smiled at Catriona, as if waiting for someone to make introductions. Catriona looked to Anthony, feeling utterly out of her element. They hadn't yet discussed how to properly introduce herself to others whom she met while out and about. Yet it felt as though the ladies were just waiting for a reason to say something.

Especially the younger two. One of them, Catriona noticed, glanced over at Lord Milington and batted her lashes. The younger of the two raised her fan, as if to hide her face.

Anthony stepped forward and bowed formally to the trio.

"What a pleasure to see you, Lady Ashmore," Anthony said. Then, he turned towards Catriona. "Miss Beaumont, may I introduce the Countess of Ashington, and her daughters, Lady Josette and Lady Rosalie."

Catriona offered a curtsey to the three ladies.

"A pleasure," she said, smiling politely.

The two younger ladies inspected her openly.

"The pleasure is all ours," the eldest said. "I have heard we have a new lady soon to be introduced to the *ton*. Miss Beaumont, it will be a pleasure to attend your presentation."

"You have such a lovely hat," Lady Josette said sweetly, "but are you not aware that white roses are out this Season?"

Catriona stared at the woman. There was no question that there was malice behind the innocent-sounding question. Was the woman trying to upset her or waiting for her to do something unladylike she could report back to the *ton*?

"I believe roses are never out, Lady Josette," Catriona said, with perfect composure. "Roses are the finest of flowers, in my opinion, and suitable all year around."

The two younger ladies snickered.

"Well, I do believe we ought to be going. We were on our way to our carriage," the countess said. "What a pleasure to meet you, Miss Beaumont. Have a good day."

"Yes, have a good day, *Lord Milington*," Lady Josette said pointedly, staring him right in the face.

But Lady Rosalie only gave a nod before all three turned on their heels and walked away.

Catriona was dumbstruck by the encounter. However, it didn't take a genius to see that Anthony, Bridget, and Lord Milington all looked extremely unsettled. They hadn't said much at all during the exchange, and she swore that Lord Milington had been actively looking for ways *not* to attract the attention of Lady Josette.

Whatever he had done, it hadn't worked.

She wondered if that meant there was some reason to be worried about the three women. They had approached and talked to her before she had been presented. Was this the kind of thing Lady Spencer was so worried about?

Either way, what worried *Catriona* the most was the way the countess had smiled at her at first. She knew it was a fake smile, the same insincere one she had seen many times on the faces of people who came to the orphanage to find someone to adopt. It was an attempt to keep the older children from losing hope.

And she doubted the woman meant well by it, and the younger pair had been even worse. However, she pushed the thought aside as Anthony redirected everyone's attention back to the swans.

Catriona threw her bread into the water, letting all of her worries go with it. She had no reason to worry there was something amiss with the chance meeting. She put her discomfort down to the fact she had been taken by surprise and had never expected to be approached by anyone in the park.

Eventually, when the bread supply was exhausted, they continued their stroll. It seemed to Catriona that the appearance of the Ashmore ladies had seriously dampened the conversation. Plus, every now and then, she caught Anthony and Lord Milington sharing looks of concern, which she could not decipher. She put her mind to enjoying the rest of their time in the park, and was disappointed when it was time to return to their separate carriages and go home.

"It has been a wonderful day, Miss Beaumont," Lord Milington said once they arrived back at the carriages. "I am glad to have had a chance to spend it with you. I wish you a good day."

"And yourself, Lord Milington," Catriona said, smiling warmly at him. It was with regret that she allowed him to help her into the carriage and prepare to take his leave as Bridget and Anthony followed her in.

"Well . . . that was certainly a lovely day," Catriona said. "It was quite lovely weather, wasn't it?"

"Yes, it was," Bridget said, absent-mindedly.

Anthony said nothing. Catriona could only wonder in silence what in the world had made them so subdued.

## Chapter Fifteen

The next morning, Catriona woke with thoughts of Lord Milington consuming her mind. He had been such a gentleman the day before while they were at the park. In part, she wondered if it was because they had been seen together in public and he wanted to be sure Lady Spencer couldn't chastise her for doing something improperly.

She also thought about the interesting run-in with the Ashmores, wondering if her family were suspicious that it had been so short.

However, she was more concerned with thinking about Lord Milington, how handsome he was, as well as kind. She couldn't stop dwelling on how he had offered to dance with her when she had trouble following the country reel and the cotillion. Catriona had really wanted to dance the waltz with him, but she didn't dare raise Lady Spencer's ire by suggesting it.

Whatever was to happen next in her life, she knew Lord Milington fit the image of a perfect Prince Charming in her mind.

Frantic knocking at the door to her bedchamber interrupted her thoughts. With a groan, Catriona got up out of bed. Upon answering the door, she found a frantic Alice standing there.

"I've been informed by Bridget that I'm to get you ready with the greatest speed."

Catriona's stomach lurched with dread on hearing that, and what Alice said next just made things worse.

"The entire family is waiting for you in the pink parlor. We *must* hurry!"

With that, Alice hurried her into the room. They picked the lilac morning dress since it was easily accessible. Off her nightclothes came, and the more they hurried, the more Catriona was convinced something must be awfully wrong.

She couldn't imagine that Bridget would ask her to get ready in such a hurried manner unless something important needed to be addressed immediately.

Once she was ready, she had Alice give her opinion on the outfit quickly.

"I think it'll be perfect for what you need. Now, hurry. Go."

With that, Catriona made her way to the pink parlor. The fact there were multiple parlors in the house had stunned her upon her first arrival. But the more time she had spent getting to know the manor, the easier it was to differentiate between them. The pink parlor was reserved for only the most serious of matters in the morning, or morning tea, depending on Lady Spencer's mood recently.

She stepped into the parlor, and everyone looked in her direction.

Lady Spencer held a handkerchief to her mouth, as if something had seriously upset her. Judging by the way Lady Spencer had been acting when Catriona did anything she didn't like, this wasn't the most alarming thing, though. In fact, Lady Bridget looked rather pathetic.

Then, she got a chance to look at Eleanor. Even the unshakeable dowager viscountess appeared shaken today, with her eyes scanning Catriona up and down, as if to catch anything they had previously missed. It was all very troubling.

She noticed that Anthony was holding something in his hands, but he did not look up at Catriona.

The silence was utterly unbearable.

Thankfully, it was broken when Bridget took Catriona by the hand and guided her towards a seat.

"Anthony, how could you? This could utterly *ruin* Catriona's reputation!" Lady Spencer's seething whisper did not help her to feel any better.

Something terrible had happened, and her stomach dropped.

Anthony stepped forward.

"I think it's about time we all calmed down so that we don't send Catriona to the floor again," he said, palms upward.

Everyone took a few moments to compose themselves out, and even Lady Spencer calmed down. Though, whatever the matter was, it was far more serious than Catriona had originally thought. She'd imagined someone had come to call on her. Now, she realized, the air was far too tense for it to be that alone.

Anthony locked eyes with her.

"Unfortunately, Catriona, it appears that your name is being dragged through the scandal sheets," he said, holding up the paper in his hand. "'It has been reported that the late Viscount Beaumore's daughter was spotted at Richmond Park,' it says. However, it goes on to say that the reason why the lady hasn't yet been presented to the *ton* is because . . . she is extremely plain."

Catriona put a hand to her mouth to stifle a gasp.

How could they call her plain? She may not have been able to grow up as other ladies of nobility had, but she thought herself quite pretty, nonetheless. Even Bridget thought the pale blue dress had done wonders for her eyes.

It took everything in her to keep the tears now welling in her eyes from falling down her cheeks. This was not good. Not good at all. Who would have the gall to spread such rumors when they didn't even know her?

"This is all your fault, Anthony," Lady Spencer said. "You brought an outsider, Lord Milington, into our house while we've been training Catriona to be a proper lady. If any person has any interest in compromising her name like this in the scandal sheets, it is him!"

"Margaret, I would appreciate it if you would keep Hamish out of this matter," Anthony said. "He's an honorable gentleman. If I believed him capable of doing something like this, I would not have asked him to accompany us to the park, nor would I have invited him for dinner the other night. But I accept that this is entirely my fault. It was my idea to go to the park, and I did not count on some rather . . . condescending ladies approaching us at the park. I know of only one way to solve our predicament."

Catriona looked up at Anthony, half in awe at his ability to stay calm, but she knew who he meant by 'condescending ladies.' *Was this why everyone looked so worried when the Ashmores came to introduce themselves to me?*

"And what would that be, Anthony?" she asked, amazed she was able to hold her tone steady. There was still a wealth of tears ready to fall, but knowing her family was willing to put everything aside to right the scandal was helping her feel more at ease.

"You must be presented to High Society as soon as possible," Anthony said. "I know this is not what you were expecting. It was not exactly what we were expecting either. But now, that is our only hope. Margaret, I trust you can arrange for Mr. Jones to come and teach Catriona how to dance properly?"

"I consider it my duty," Lady Spencer said.

"I can take care of all of the invitations," Bridget said. "I have meant to make the rounds to my friends and visit them all lately anyway. Catriona, perhaps you could help me decide on the theme and colors for the ball?"

"I would like that, thank you, Bridget."

It was a consolation prize, she knew, but Bridget actively seeking her contribution for something so important to everyone was good. Catriona wanted to be part of squashing the nasty comments. Extremely plain? She didn't think so.

If this was how Anthony thought they could best put a stop to wagging tongues, then she was going to put her trust in him. After all, Anthony and Bridget, and everyone else in the room, had grown up in Society. To fix the matter, she would have to take their advice. She had never felt the effects of such a powerful rumor so acutely, until today.

"The modiste helped you to choose proper ball gowns, yes, Catriona?" Eleanor spoke as she turned her head to look at Catriona, who nodded.

"Have any arrived yet?"

"The ivory one," Catriona said. "It is, I believe, Lady Spencer's intention for me to wear that particular gown for my presentation."

"Good. That's at least one less thing we'll have to worry about over the next few days," the dowager said. "This isn't going to be easy, but if any family can make such a ball happen in such a short amount of time, I do believe it will be us."

"If you'll all excuse me, I shall go and write to Mr. Jones at once," Lady Spencer said. "I beg your pardon."

With that, Lady Spencer left the room.

The air felt less tense without her. Catriona wondered if the lady had the same effect on everyone else, eliciting an intense feeling of shame. Lady Spencer was always so critical of Catriona; did Anthony sometimes feel that same pressure?

But Bridget had already assured her that it was how Lady Spencer behaved to any new women in the family. It wasn't entirely reassuring to know that, though, not now there might be a scandal brewing to do with Catriona.

"Come. I think you and I ought to start on the invitations," Bridget said. "Anthony, I trust you have the rest of the details attended to?"

"Yes. The ball ought to be held no later than three weeks from now. We need to keep on top of this situation."

With that, Bridget took Catriona out of the room.

"Who could have spread such a rumor?" Catriona asked her as they went into the library, where there was a large writing table. "And what do they hope to gain by it?"

"One of the other ladies at the park may have been jealous," her ladyship speculated, "but I cannot say for certain. The only thing I do know for certain is that Anthony was right to be worried when the Ashmores came over. It seemed too deliberate. They are known to be . . . gossipers, but I never suspected they would be so mean as to say that someone hadn't been presented to the *ton* because she is plain."

Catriona frowned deeply, and then she remembered that one of the Ashmore ladies had directed most of her attention towards Lord Milington. Perhaps it was not her looks they had been jealous of, but the attention he was clearly paying to her.

She pushed all that aside as she and Bridget sat down together and began to write out a guest list and plan their invitations. As they worked, Catriona admitted to herself that she felt almost completely overwhelmed by the pressure now.

They soon decided on a simple, traditional style for the invitations, with Bridget writing out each invitation by hand with perfect penmanship. Catriona was glad of it. Being from an orphanage, she hadn't had a chance to perfect her handwriting.

"I can handle it from here," Bridget said. "Go and see if any other dresses from the modiste have arrived. I don't want you to feel as if you're going to be stuck wearing the same dresses, though I can tell you like the blue and lilac the most."

Catriona managed a smile.

"I wish to thank you and Anthony for all that you're doing to help me adjust to my new life, Bridget," she said quietly before walking out.

## Chapter Sixteen

Hamish watched as his valet selected the clothing from the large closet in the corner of the room and laid it out on the bed for his master's approval. The man had already helped him shave that morning, an ordeal Hamish always struggled with. Now, it was time to get dressed for the day.

After yesterday's incident in the park with the Ashmores, he was dreading having to join his family for breakfast at Mildenwoode Manor. But he dressed suitably, in buff breeches, a claret-colored coat, and high-top riding boots.

Donning his top hat and grabbing his cane, Hamish started towards the door. He could only hope that today's breakfast was not going to come with the usual pushing and pressure towards a marriage with Lady Josette Ashmore. But he didn't hold out much hope.

"The newspaper, my lord," said the butler, handing him the paper.

"Thank you, that'll be a good way to distract myself on the journey," he said with a grateful nod, glancing down at the latest edition of the London *Times*.

Scanning the paper as he sat in the carriage, his thoughts were actually on Miss Beaumont. She had looked so beautiful the day before in that pale-blue dress. Shades of blue suited her well.

He couldn't deny that he enjoyed her company too. She could bring light to any conversation, and the fact she was not afraid to broach more sensitive topics endeared her to him.

No other lady had ever thought to share her love of reading with him before. It was something they could potentially enjoy together. He found himself admiring the way Catriona had made the best of her limited free time at the orphanage by finding something she liked despite the poor way she was treated.

As he was thinking about how terrible it was for *anyone* to be considered worthless when they were a mere thirteen years old—*thirteen, for crying out loud*—he came across the latest scandal sheet.

The headline caught his attention. As he read the article, his stomach twisted in fury. Once again, the gossips had their knives out, this time for Catriona.

He crumpled the paper and hurled it away, unable to read another word of the foul lie. He thought back to how Lady Josette had seen him with Miss Beaumont in the park. She and her family now no doubt considered Miss Beaumont a threat to the marriage that everyone except Hamish himself wanted. Here was the evidence—they had taken that gossip right to the scandal sheets themselves.

It required a few good, deep breaths to quell his fury as his carriage finally arrived at Mildenwoode Manor.

The butler showed him to the drawing room, and he attempted to leave his thoughts and worries about Miss Beaumont's reputation at the carriage door. This was not the time nor the place to indicate that he had feelings for anyone else. He didn't want to give the duke a chance to pressure him into feeling as if Lady Josette was the right woman for him. And he certainly didn't want to hear another lecture on how proper it would be to marry her for business connections alone when he felt there was something not altogether above board hiding in the earl's ledgers.

He smiled upon seeing his mother in the drawing room. Sitting across from her, his father had a cup of tea already in front of him. That didn't bother Hamish, for it meant that His Grace had already begun to get ready and wound up for the day, and he sent up a quiet prayer that he would be able to get through the breakfast without his father bringing up the arranged marriage.

"Ah, Hamish, what a lovely day it is to see you," the Duchess of Mildenwoode said.

"I'm happy to have been able to get here for breakfast," Hamish said. "Thank you for inviting me."

Breakfast was served a moment later.

After the servants had left the room, and as Hamish was buttering a piece of toast to enjoy, his father cleared his throat.

"I believe it would be best for you to secure a match with Lady Josette before the end of the month," the duke said.

Hamish glanced at his mother, who appeared immediately pained at the thought of arranging a marriage for Hamish. On the other hand, he could tell his father wished to be completely honest with him, and probably for Hamish to be honest with his father.

If that was the case, then he decided that it would probably be best to tell the duke he wanted nothing to do with the marriage, while keeping his feelings for Miss Beaumont from entering into consideration for now.

"I'm sorry, Father, but I do not trust the Earl of Ashington," Hamish said. "I also have no desire to marry Lady Josette. She is certainly a match for one of the lords, but I do not believe I am the right one for her. I find her company unbearable, and I would certainly suffer for it in a marriage. It is not even about finding love, Father; it is about being able to live with the woman I marry for the rest of my life."

Though he didn't know exactly what to expect, he knew his father was most likely not happy about what he'd just said. There was really nothing more to say, but a pit opened in his stomach as he waited for his father to respond.

"You're being foolish, Hamish, something I thought was below you," his father said.

Watching his father's nostrils flare as he spoke, though, made Hamish doubt that his father really believed he was being foolish. What he felt was *more* likely was that his father couldn't believe Hamish dared to speak against something that would have been a huge boon to the business . . . but nothing else.

"I'm sorry, Father, but that is exactly what I think," Hamish said.

"The Earl of Ashington has been a friend of ours for many years," his father continued, "and he is completely trustworthy. I cannot understand why you would throw away such a good opportunity like this based on a few meaningless emotions."

"It's not on a few meaningless emotions," Hamish quietly said. "I swear, my gut is telling me otherwise. It would not be a good move."

He rose to his feet as he spoke, hoping to the heavens that his father wouldn't continue pressing his argument. However, knowing his father, Hamish had a feeling it would be best for him to leave sooner rather than later. He honestly didn't want an argument over breakfast, and there was no denying that the conversation had rather quickly evolved into an argument, not a conversation between reasonable people.

As his father opened his mouth to say more, Hamish glanced at his mother. She had always avoided making his father angry, and now he and the duke were starting to argue, he saw something in her face. She was quietly *begging* him not to continue. Aware that she always wanted to keep the peace, Hamish decided that, for now, the conversation was not worth continuing.

He stepped away from the table.

"I best be on my way. Good day, Father, Mother. Thank you for breakfast."

He walked out of the room without another word, but he was well aware that if he had continued with the argument, his father would have been angered by something he said. He feared seeing the duke grow very upset and angry while his mother was in the room.

She had never deserved the way his father treated them, but then again, what else could be expected from a loveless marriage?

The rest of the day passed quietly, and Hamish later met Anthony at White's club that evening for drinks. But Hamish reckoned they weren't there to celebrate their upcoming joint business venture. After the way the scandal sheets had treated

Miss Beaumont, he had a feeling Anthony wanted to drown some sorrows.

Hamish didn't mind the sound of that kind of a meeting.

As he walked into the club, he found Anthony sitting at a table, alone, with a glass in his hand and a solemn look on his face.

"I see we both have had some rather upsetting news today," Hamish said as he sat down across the table from his friend.

"I blame myself for that scandal sheet, Hamish," Anthony said. "It was *my* idea to go to the park. I should have known there were going to be people in the *ton* who are threatened by Miss Beaumont's arrival. I should have kept her at the house. She might have enjoyed a day in the gardens just as much."

"Anthony, if anyone is to blame for that scandal sheet, it's not you. It's the Ashmores. If it weren't for them being such . . . *malicious* gossipers, I don't think you'd have to worry about any scandal sheets," Hamish said.

"Why must they be such gossipers, anyway?" Anthony looked up at him, clearly a little lost in his drink already. "What do they gain from trying to damage Catriona before she's even been presented?"

"Anthony, I don't think we'll ever figure out why they do what they do," he said. "But, for now, I think the best thing we can do is drown our sorrows. I'll buy the next round of drinks."

He signaled a waiter, and upon the arrival of the drinks, he looked Anthony in the eyes.

"We could dwell on their machinations all day long, but it does us no good. What *will* do us good, I believe, is to forget them for the night." Hamish said. "So, instead, let us talk of something else, something that brings us both joy."

Anthony looked up and nodded. "Agreed."

They clinked their glasses together before reminiscing about their college days. It had been many years since then, but discussing their youthful antics kept them entertained all evening.

After all, with so many other problems weighing on them both, Hamish knew they'd both be better off for it. It also lifted his spirits to see Anthony forget the troubles that came with the *ton* and their scandal sheets.

The entire time they drank, however, Hamish could not stop thinking about what his father was trying to make him do. To marry Lady Josette would be to resign himself to a loveless business arrangement with a woman he could barely stand. After watching his parents' marriage at close quarters for years, that was the last thing he wanted.

In his alcoholic stupor, Hamish quietly began to wonder why his mother had never fought the marriage to his father when it was clear she was utterly lonely and unhappy in her situation. Had his father forced her into the marriage the way he was trying to force Hamish into a marriage with Lady Josette?

## Chapter Seventeen

Two days after the scandal sheet ripped through London, Catriona stood in the hallway of the manor, wondering what awaited her that day. So far, there had been full two days of dancing and etiquette lessons, which she found both strenuous and troublesome. Mornings, when she was wide awake, were not too bad. But the longer the family worked on making sure she would be presentable for the ton, the harder it was for her to remember everything she was supposed to.

Taking a deep breath, she continued down the hallway, clutching her shaking hands together. What lessons awaited her today in the ballroom? Lady Spencer had arranged for Mr. Jones to come daily to teach her all the dances she needed to know. But Catriona was struggling with them all.

As she entered the ballroom, she saw Lady Spencer and Mr. Jones discussing something in one corner. Upon the door opening, they stopped and turned to see who had arrived. When Lady Spencer locked eyes with Catriona, the conversation immediately died.

Catriona's stomach knotted up. From the way the discussion had stopped, she knew what the topic had been—herself. It struck Catriona then that Lady Spencer must be paying Mr. Jones a lot of money to keep him sweet—and quiet—in order to protect Catriona's reputation.

"Come, Miss Beaumont. Take your position."

Mr. Jones motioned her forward, and immediately assumed his position for the dance.

It didn't help knowing that Lady Spencer, Eleanor, Mrs. Mills, and Bridget were all sitting on the other side of the ballroom watching her every move. That, and Mr. Jones' stern mannerisms, made her nervous. As a result, poor Mr. Jones' feet were victim to many a trampling.

Catriona quietly wished that she could have been dancing with Lord Milington instead of Mr. Jones. He had made it seem so easy when they had danced a cotillion after dinner the other evening. His trick of blocking out the rest of the ballroom and focusing on her partner didn't work with Mr. Jones as it had with him.

Mr. Jones was paid to interrupt her thoughts to correct her slouching shoulders, or the way she had extended her arm, or anything that was a hair out of place. He wanted her to be the picture-perfect lady while dancing, which she certainly understood the need for. That was why Lady Spencer had hired the best to teach her how to dance.

However, the more they practiced, the more Catriona felt she was utterly failing to grasp his directions.

As the set came to an end, Lady Spencer let out a heavy sigh.

"Catriona shall never be ready at this rate!"

"Margaret, don't be so hard on her," Eleanor replied. "She's been under a lot of pressure and shall be until her ball. I do believe she is doing well, considering how much we have been trying to teach her in such a short time. It is only natural that she won't grasp some things as quickly as others."

"The bright side," Mr. Jones chimed in, "is that she is indeed getting better. My feet are less sore this morning. And, Miss Beaumont, I can see that you are making a great effort to take into consideration what I point out. That makes all the difference, however slight it may seem to begin with. You are at a disadvantage when it comes to dancing, as you are learning so much too quickly. But believe me, you are progressing."

"Thank you, Mr. Jones."

To hear him say it, despite his stern manner and the way he insisted on correcting every tiny mistake while she was on the floor, made Catriona feel less upset about her progress.

"Well, I do believe that is all we have time for today," Mr. Jones continued. "Miss Beaumont, it is a pleasure to dance with you. I hope you will consider everything I have pointed out to improve your dancing. Until our next lesson," he added, bowing low.

"Until then, Mr. Jones."

Catriona watched as he readied to leave. Lady Spencer thanked him personally again, perhaps because she felt bad about how Catriona was struggling so much with some of the dances. Still, it was nice for Catriona to know there were some people who understood how much she had to learn in a brief time, and that it was far more than she had ever had to learn before about anything.

After lunch, Bridget sat with Catriona in the pink parlor. They were going over the RSVPs that had arrived in response to their invitations for the ball, and Catriona's stomach knotted at seeing just how many acceptances had come back.

"Is it normal for so many people to attend a ball like this, Bridget?" Catriona looked over at the woman, suddenly unsure.

"Usually, yes," Bridget said without looking up from the stack of envelopes in her hand. "And, in this case, it is a good thing. It means the scandal sheet has either intrigued everyone or they have decided not to pay attention to it and they wish to make their own judgment of you. I cannot tell which is better."

Catriona nodded.

As she continued to go through the RSVPs, she came across the acceptance card from the Countess of Ashington and her daughters, Lady Josette and Lady Rosalie.

Catriona's stomach knotted up even more on seeing their names.

"Who's that RSVP from, Catriona?" Bridget looked up upon seeing she had gone quiet. "Catriona?"

"It's from the Ashmores . . . they say they'll be coming." She gulped hard. "They were the ones at the park, yes? The ladies that you, Anthony, and Lord Milington were all rather nervous about introducing me to."

"Yes," Bridget said. "I'm not surprised they're coming, though I wish I didn't have to invite them. But they're rather prominent members of the *ton,* so its unavoidable."

Bridget now took Catriona's hand and squeezed it tightly.

"The best thing you can do is to pretend they mean you no ill will. Anthony didn't want to invite them, either, but Lady Spencer *insisted* it would be bad manners to snub them. For now, all you need to worry about is making sure that you're ready with your dancing and such for the ball. All right?" Bridget pulled her hand away as she spoke.

"I know you're right, Bridget," Catriona said, "but that's much easier said than done. You and all of the other ladies who will be there have had years to learn all of this. I'm having to learn it all in a matter of a few weeks. It's . . . it's not easy."

"It wasn't easy to learn it all over the years, either, Catriona," Bridget said. "Any *sensible* woman of the *ton* who knew what sort of a childhood you'd had would understand there is a lot for you to take in. To learn it all so quickly and to pull it off successfully is a feat that should be rewarded not looked down upon. Unfortunately, I do not have the influence to change things."

"I appreciate you helping me, though, Bridget," Catriona said. "Especially with Lady Spencer. It seems she's still fixated on making sure I remember *everything* properly by the time the ball comes around. I've given up on knowing *everything* by then. I'm trying to make sure I know the basics, and anything else I pick up in the next few days will be a bonus."

"That's a good way to do it. It can't be easy, I know," Bridget replied. "Now . . . why don't we mark the Ashmores down as attending? Now, I shall tell you a little more about some of the other people who are coming, so you're not entirely in the dark. I believe there are plenty of more sensible ladies of my acquaintance with whom you will be safe conversing, aside from the required pleasantries, of course."

"Does that mean I'm going to have to meet the Ashmores again?"

"Yes, probably, but this time, there will be more restraint on what they can say and do, being guests in our house," Lady Beaumore said. "I think this is the best place to have to face them again . . . if you must."

Catriona stifled a snicker but failed. Knowing Lady Spencer wasn't in the room made it a little easier to feel comfortable around Bridget, who smiled at the snicker.

"See? You'll be fine, Catriona. You're doing better at holding things back, though I cannot blame you for laughing when it's just the two of us. There will be plenty of time for you to see what Society is really like at close quarters. Now, let us get on with sorting out these acceptances. I have a lot over here that we haven't even *touched*."

Catriona nodded.

Catriona wondered why Lady Spencer, who appeared well aware of what kind of trouble the Ashmore family could stir up, had insisted on the Ashmores being invited to her coming out ball. If someone was mean, then why invite them to your party? She sighed. That was another thing she was learning about the *ton*—it did things its own way.

She also vividly recalled the unfriendly way Miss Josette Ashmore had behaved towards her in the park after seeing her escorted by Lord Milington. Clearly, the lady had an interest in him. Since Lord Milington had done nothing to return the attention, Catriona suspected the affection was one-sided. Could the lady be jealous of her?

"Bridget . . . is it normal for a woman to pay more attention to a man than the person she's just been introduced to?" She looked up from the last of her envelopes.

"If you're still thinking about the way Lady Josette behaved towards Lord Milington, I think you can forget about it," Bridget said, not looking up. "Lord Milington has never been interested in the Ashmore ladies, though many other men would crawl through the sewers of London to retrieve Lady Josette's handkerchief if she dropped it there if they thought they would earn a chance to court her. I cannot see why so many men wish to court those two ladies other than the money prestige it would bring them."

"That's not entirely reassuring, but thank you, Bridget."

"I try," Bridget said, finally looking up. "I've seen Lady Josette flutter her eyelashes at butlers before now, Catriona. You have no reason to worry about her."

That caught Catriona's attention, but before she could ask anything more about it, Bridget ticked off the last of the RSVPs, making sure everyone was marked correctly on her sheet of names.

"Well, that's all for the moment," Bridget said. "We're done for the day."

# Chapter Eighteen

The last several days had kept Hamish quite busy. Business matters had needed overseeing, and, after having drinks with Anthony, he was quite glad to have something to keep him away from home for a while. He hadn't heard anything from his father since their argument, and Hamish was not concerned by it.

He'd rather keep his father at arm's length for as long as possible. There was something unnerving about the way his father wanted to marry him off to Lady Josette that simply didn't sit right . . . especially not now he had voiced his opinion on the matter and learned that his father disagreed with him.

Then again, even though his father now knew how Hamish felt about the situation, he didn't seriously expect him to back off. He'd tried twice to tell the duke that Lady Josette simply wasn't the kind of woman he wanted to marry, and his father *still* hadn't accepted it.

He worried that if he were to go against the desired marriage and do what he wanted instead, that his father would find a way to take revenge. He might try to ruin the reputation of any one Hamish might court and wish to marry. Hamish wasn't sure he could take such a risk, not with Miss Beaumont's coming out ball being so close. Not for Anthony's sake, at least.

He arrived at Beaumore Manor to discuss a potential business deal with Anthony, glad once more to have something of his own that his father had no control over. If the venture could be agreed upon, Hamish was confident it would succeed, and he would be almost independent of his father's grip. Then, he could potentially do whatever he wanted, without fear of consequences.

The butler let him in and gave him a deep bow.

"I shall tell his lordship you are here, my lord," the man said.

With that, Hamish was left alone in the hallway for a few minutes, waiting to be admitted. Standing there, he became aware of faint music coming from the ballroom. He imagined Miss Beaumont was having some sort of dancing lesson. As much as Hamish yearned to dance with her again, sadly, he knew it was not his place today.

A few moments later, Anthony emerged from the ballroom. That about sealed it for Hamish.

Miss Beaumont was having a dancing lesson *right now*.

What concerned Hamish immediately, however, was how worried Anthony looked.

"Catriona and Mr. Jones are going through the waltz now," Anthony said, unprompted. "I don't think things are going too well, and I'm at my wit's end, Hamish. Catriona's ball is in *three days' time*! What shall we do if she cannot dance?"

"When I danced with her, I found Miss Beaumont to be very light on her feet, Anthony," Hamish said, puzzled. "Why is she struggling so much now?"

"I think you've just solved our problem, Hamish," he said. "I hate to put you on the spot like this, but would you mind stepping in as Catriona's dance partner? Perhaps we have simply been coming at it from the wrong angle . . ."

"I would not mind at all, Anthony. In fact, it would be my *pleasure,"* Hamish grinned, mighty pleased with himself.

Anthony laughed a little and walked with him to the ballroom. Upon their arrival, Hamish was actually shocked to see Mr. Jones and Catriona struggling through the waltz. She was trampling on the dance master's feet as if she were drunk, and Mr. Jones was clearly unhappy about it. The red of Miss Beaumont's cheeks showed how embarrassing she found the whole situation.

Anthony cleared his throat to get everyone's attention.

"Lord Milington has offered to step in as Catriona's dance partner for a few minutes," Anthony announced. "Perhaps a change of partner shall best serve us?"

"Not for the waltz! Catriona is not courting Lord Milington," Lady Spencer exclaimed.

"I agree with Lady Spencer on this matter," Mr. Jones said. "The waltz is one of the most romantic dances ever, but it is proper only for courting or married couples, in my opinion."

"Lord Milington danced the cotillion with Miss Beaumont the other night, Mr. Jones," Anthony said, "and she was perfectly fine with him. It is not a matter of whether or not they are courting. Since Lord Milington is not a teacher, this will allow you to see her technique as it would be on the dance floor at the ball itself."

Neither Lady Spencer nor Mr. Jones seemed to have an argument for that. Since that was the case, Hamish turned his attention to Miss Beaumont.

He couldn't deny he felt ecstatic at being able to dance with her again. However, for Lady Spencer's sake, he decided to do his best to avoid showing how he felt. Especially since Lady Spencer might still blame him for Miss Beaumont's name appearing in the scandal sheets.

Hamish couldn't help but smile warmly as he came to stand in front of Miss Beaumont. He bowed, and she dipped into a flawless curtsey, which at least seemed to ease the tension in the room.

"May I have this dance, Miss Beaumont?"

"I would be honored, Lord Milington."

As she accepted his request, he couldn't help noticing that her cheeks flushed bright crimson. A thrill shot through him. Either he was imagining she was just as excited to dance with him as he was with her, or she was flummoxed by all the fuss over her dancing. Either way, he couldn't believe his luck.

He offered her his hand, and she took it. He placed his hand on her waist, and she rested hers on his shoulder, just as she was meant to.

"Mrs. Mills, are you ready with the pianoforte?" Mr. Jones turned to Mrs. Mills, who nodded. "All right then. One, two, three . . ."

Mr. Jones continued to count for another measure as Mrs. Mills started to play the music. Since Hamish already knew how to dance the waltz, he moved easily about the floor, guiding Catriona. But he could feel the tension in her body, her shoulders had no give, and it felt almost as if she was struggling to keep up with him.

He leaned in close to her ear again.

"Do you remember what I told you the last time we danced?"

"That it's all right to forget everything except the two of us on the floor . . . I remember," Miss Beaumont whispered. "But how can I concentrate when everyone is judging me?"

"Then give them a reason to question that judgment, Miss Beaumont."

He offered a smile as he pulled away, and she raised her brows at him, but appeared to take his words into consideration. Instead of trying to keep up with everything Mr. Jones had been criticizing about her technique, she relaxed into Hamish's lead.

He watched with pleasure as she started to keep up without him needing to say anything. In fact, the more she relaxed, the better she danced. It appeared that his tip was helping her again.

Eventually, the music came to an end. Hamish glided to a halt as he helped Miss Beaumont do the same. He sensed she had wanted to keep dancing, and he didn't blame her. The way they complimented each other simply felt natural to him, and there were plenty of other reasons for them to continue dancing with each other.

"Oh, that was just lovely!"

The dowager viscountess started to clap as she spoke. This was followed by everyone else also clapping, giving the pair a round of applause as Hamish brought Miss Beaumont back to the side of the ballroom.

As he let her return to her spot, Hamish realized one person was not clapping, Lady Spencer, of course. Hamish thought she must be sulking because Hamish had been able to get Miss

Beaumont to dance beautifully—despite the fact they were not courting.

Hamish wanted to remedy that situation as soon as possible, but he knew he'd have to be patient.

"Thank you for the dance, Lord Milington," Miss Beaumont said.

"It was my pleasure, Miss Beaumont. All my pleasure." He smiled at her as he dipped into a bow. "Now, if you'll excuse us, Anthony and I have some business to discuss."

He looked over at Anthony, who nodded. As they walked out of the ballroom, he heard Mr. Jones and Lady Spencer commenting on Miss Beaumont's form, but they were a lot less critical than previously. Well, Mr. Jones was, at least. Lady Spencer seemed irritated, perhaps because Catriona had been able to dance the waltz so seamlessly with him but not with Mr. Jones. How satisfying but deeply inappropriate!

Then again, Lady Spencer would do anything to be sure that Miss Beaumont was the picture of perfection without a breath of scandal to her name. The fact that it had appeared in the scandal sheets after their visit to Richmond Park had probably thrown Lady Spencer's plans into disarray, in her eyes, putting the family reputation in jeopardy.

It wasn't until they were down the hallway and halfway to the office that Anthony said anything to Hamish.

"That was absolutely lovely, that waltz," he said. "Thank you so much for doing that, even though I put you on the spot. I was just . . . oh, I cannot thank you enough!"

"It was nothing, Anthony," Hamish insisted. "She's a lovely dancer, and I was happy to dance with her. I look forward to dancing with her again at the ball, though I am not sure Lady Spencer will approve."

"Lady Spencer wanted to blame you for the way Catriona's name was dragged into the scandal sheets," Anthony revealed. "I told her to leave you out of it. If I had been worried that you were going to do something like that, I would have approached and asked you about your intentions. But you are the picture of a gentleman. Even if you would rather not marry Lady Josette."

That made them both laugh.

No proper gentleman in his right mind would want to marry Lady Josette for her personality. And since Hamish was the kind of man who wanted to marry for love, they both knew there was little chance he would be happy in a marriage to Lady Josette Ashmore.

"I do appreciate your willingness to defend my honor," Hamish said. "My father would have probably approved of my dragging her name through the sheets if he thought I had anything to do with it. I don't think he's quite realized there is a new lady in the *ton* whom everyone is wondering about."

"I'd like to keep it that way," Anthony remarked. "Your father has done enough damage to your own happiness so far. I'd hate him to learn how happy you are in Catriona's company."

They entered Anthony's study, and Anthony poured them some drinks. Meanwhile, Hamish dwelled on the dance lesson; he could no longer deny the electric connection between himself and Miss Beaumont.

And he certainly hoped his father would continue to ignore Miss Beaumont's existence.

# Chapter Nineteen

The next morning, Catriona didn't get out of bed immediately. Instead, her thoughts were consumed with Lord Milington. Again. She knew it was probably not good to be so obsessed with the idea of courting him, but she couldn't deny she was starting to develop feelings for him.

Why else would her cheeks glow red both times he'd asked her to dance? Or when he was simply near her? Why did she feel butterflies in her stomach when they were together?

She certainly couldn't deny it any longer, not after the way she had been able to dance with him so easily the day before in the ballroom. She had to admit that Mr. Jones always made her feel a little unwelcome in the ballroom. Perhaps it was just because he always had to critique her form or because of his stern manner. But Lord Milington made her feel as though whatever she did was good enough.

His tip to pretend that they were the only two in the ballroom had helped her tremendously both times they were on the floor. It had also probably helped that they had been able to dance without interruption.

She quietly wished he would dance with her at the ball.

Her thoughts were interrupted by the sound of knocking at her bedchamber door. Despite how comfortable she was in bed and how much she wanted to continue thinking about Lord Milington and the way he made her feel, she called, "Come in."

Alice entered.

"Good morning, Alice." Catriona smiled.

"Good morning. Lady Bridget has informed me that we have a busy day ahead. It's time for you to get ready for breakfast, Catriona," Alice said with a smile.

"All right."

With that, Catriona moved aside so that Alice could get to work.

Catriona bathed, and afterward, Alice brushed her hair out into a shining mass at the vanity.

"Are you excited about having breakfast with the family, Catriona?"

"Yes . . . though my stomach is anything but," she said with a laugh. "Is my own family a reason enough to feel I cannot eat much this morning?"

"Well, you have an unusually imposing family," Alice said. "Come on, then. Let us choose a nice dress."

They eventually settled on a pale-green morning dress, and Alice soon helped her into it and laced it up tightly.

"Phew! I think I can just about breathe," Catriona joked. "Thank you, Alice."

"You look lovely," Alice said with a smile. "Now, let me finish your hair and you'll be ready."

Catriona nodded, and once her hair was done, she went downstairs to join the family for breakfast. As she entered the room, she intensely wished her best friend could join them for breakfast for moral support.

"Good morning, everyone," Catriona said, glancing around the room and nodding and smiling at the family members gathered there.

"Good morning, Catriona," Bridget said as she sat down, with the rest of the family echoing the greeting. "Eleanor, Margaret, and Hannah will be arriving after breakfast. There's to be a final fitting with the modiste for your grand ball gown—which I believe is already here. It's always a good idea to get a final fitting at home when you're two days' away from the ball itself. There might be some last alterations to make, and this is the best time to do it."

Catriona nodded as she started to serve herself with some breakfast, though she knew it wasn't going to be easy swallowing any of it.

She could hardly believe she was going to be officially presented to the *ton* in just two days' time. It felt like only yesterday that she had discovered she was the daughter of the late Viscount Beaumore. Yet with everything she had learned since then, she felt as if her life at the orphanage was a distant dream, though she had only left a couple of months ago.

"Is it odd to be nervous about one's first ball, Bridget?" Catriona eventually voiced the question that was nagging at her. "Especially a ball where all eyes will be on me?"

"If you weren't nervous, I would be a little worried. A ball like this is a big thing for a young lady, and for the *ton*. To be properly presented after only a few months instead of years of training is almost unheard of." Bridget pursed her lips. "But I do believe that once others have learned and seen how far you've come, they'll understand why we have decided to have your coming out ball this Season instead of waiting until the next one. Margaret turned out to be right about that, after all."

Catriona nodded.

That seemed to be the end of the conversation for the time being, as Bridget and Anthony went on to talk about some business matter between them. Catriona managed to eat something, which she took as a good sign. She didn't know what kind of business the pair were discussing, but she thought she heard Lord Milington's name being mentioned. Sadly, they spoke too quietly for her to hear more, and she knew she couldn't ask despite her burning curiosity.

After breakfast, Anthony excused himself to attend to other affairs.

That left Catriona and Bridget alone in the drawing room.

"Come. The modiste will be here soon, and I think you should go and put on the ball gown ready for the fitting," Bridget told her.

"Thank you, I shall," Catriona said, eating the last of her toast and finishing her tea before rising to her feet to obey.

"Good girl. Now, hurry along. Everyone else will be here soon. We shall meet in the same room as before when you're ready."

With that, Catriona took her leave from the drawing room. To her surprise, a smiling Alice was already waiting by the door to the bedchamber.

"Lady Bridget told me to help you with your ball gown for the fitting today," Alice explained. "It's so exciting, isn't it? Not just to be attending a ball, but to be the star of the ball . . ." she added as they went into Catriona's bedchamber and shut the door behind them.

"I think I'll feel better once it's here, Alice." Catriona forced a half-chuckle as Alice helped her out of her morning dress and into the white ball gown.

After a few minutes, Catriona was ready to return to the drawing room. When she entered, the modiste and the ladies of the family were already there. Everyone stopped talking and turned to stare at her. Though she felt uncomfortable with all eyes on her as she struggled to walk across the room in the too-long skirt, Catriona was relieved to know it was one thing that would be fixed today. This was the final fitting.

"Oh, yes, the gown needs taking up, but that is easily fixed," the modiste said, looking Catriona up and down closely. "That's the only thing I can see immediately that needs work."

The modiste turned to the rest of the family for thoughts. Catriona was quite glad to see they were willing to look at the dress and give their opinions, too. If Catriona's opinion was the only one that mattered, it would never meet their high expectations.

"I think a little more lace on the sleeves would be gorgeous," Lady Spencer said. "But just a little. She doesn't need to be entirely decked out, but this dress is too . . . well, we all know the word I wish to use."

"I agree with Margaret," Bridget said. "It's a beautiful gown, but it's far too *common*, and that's what we want to avoid."

"To be fair to the modiste, I don't think this was originally meant to be the dress for my presentation ball," Catriona spoke up. "We might have originally thought it would be a good general ball gown."

"I think the lady is right," the modiste said, "but that doesn't mean we can't make it perfect. The pearl rosettes are perfectly placed, though, and I don't think any of you can argue with that one."

No one argued, which meant that one thing at least was considered quite proper.

Eleanor looked her over.

"The dress might not be ready for a ball yet, but I think you make plain look beautiful, Catriona," Eleanor said, smiling. "I'm proud to be your grandmother. Look at how far you've come in the last few weeks. From an orphan who knew nothing of how to behave in proper Society to a lady getting ready for her presentation to the *ton*. Next thing we know, you'll be married and having your own family."

Catriona felt her heart glow as Eleanor spoke. It was indeed a good day if Eleanor said she was proud of the progress Catriona had made since first learning she was part of the Beaumont family.

"I must admit that although the dress is a little plain for a coming out ball, Catriona somehow manages to make it seem quite elegant," Margaret commented. "Perhaps all we need do is find you a good pearl necklace. Accent the gown properly, and suddenly, it is not so plain, after all."

Catriona *beamed* at Margaret's praise. Her strict aunt had finally started to come around too. Lady Spencer, Aunt Margaret . . . however she was supposed to be addressed . . . she had finally started to warm to her charge. Though she may not have approved of Catriona dancing with Lord Milington, or of Lord Milington in general being around the place, Lady Spencer had finally deigned to give her a compliment.

Catriona's heart swelled; she finally had a family, and it felt far too good to be part of it.

Everyone seemed pleased with how the fitting had gone, and the modiste was going to shorten the hem so Catriona wouldn't trip over her skirts. Back in her bedchamber, Alice helped her out of the gown, and Catriona quickly redressed. From there, she went down to the garden terrace, where tea was being served to the ladies.

The conversations there focused mainly on last-minute arrangements for the ball, but Catriona could hardly focus. Excitement and nerves were finally working her to exhaustion, and by the time she arrived at her bedchamber that evening, she wanted to simply collapse onto the bed—clothes and all—and fall asleep until the ball itself!

Thankfully, Alice was on hand to help her change into her nightclothes and brushed out her hair before fastening it into loose plaits.

"Everything seems to be falling into place, Catriona," Alice said. "It's wonderful, isn't it?"

Catriona nodded, knowing no one else but Alice could ever understand why she was so nervous. Alice had come from the same orphanage as her to be her lady's maid, and her friend was the greatest help to her.

"Yes, it is, but I'm extremely nervous about the ball. What if I'm not good enough for the *ton*? What if I make a mistake and my name gets into the scandal sheets again, and not in a good way?" She sighed.

"Catriona, the best thing you can do is be yourself," Alice said. "That's what has gotten you this far already. And, besides, the worst thing you can do is present yourself as someone you're not. You may not have all of the etiquette down pat yet, but you're learning as fast as you possibly can. Under the circumstances, I don't think there is a lady in the *ton* who *wouldn't* be happy with your progress."

Alice gave her a deep look from the mirror.

"You're right." Catriona nodded. "The best thing I can do is be myself, and if that means someone doesn't want to get to know me, then *they* will be missing out. I haven't gotten this far by trying to present myself as someone everyone should wish to know . . . and I certainly won't get much further by trying to hide my past. If anyone considers growing up in an orphanage a disgrace, then I don't wish to know them, nor do I care what they think of me. Nevertheless, I want to make the best impression I can."

"That's my friend," Alice said, putting down the hairbrush. "All right . . . I think you're ready for bed. Now, you need a good night's rest. Enough worrying for the night."

Catriona nodded. "You're right, as usual, Alice."

With that, she got into the bed, and she fell asleep thinking about Lord Milington and how she could hardly wait to see him at the ball. Sadly, she knew she was unlikely to see him before then.

# Chapter Twenty

The day of Miss Beaumont's ball finally arrived, and his valet was helping Hamish get dressed for the affair. He had decided to dress as well as possible—both because it was what was expected of him and because he wanted to make a good impression on Miss Beaumont.

His dress shirt had been freshly laundered for the occasion. A white waistcoat paired with long-time coat in blue adorned his upper half, while his lower half was clothed in black satin knee-breeches and classic white stockings with clocks at the ankle (if only to make Miss Beaumont laugh a little with the absurdity of their popularity). Finally, he finished it all off with a pair of black shoes with ribbon ties and a *chapeau-bras*—and a perfectly tied cravat.

His black, crescent-shaped opera hat was perhaps his favorite part of the outfit, and he wasn't quite sure that Miss Beaumont would know it was called a *chapeau-bras.*

Not that it mattered. Either way, he could hardly hold back his excitement at being able to dance the waltz with Miss Beaumont later that night. Anthony, in the midst of their business discussion the other day, had mentioned that it would probably be a good thing for Miss Beaumont to be seen dancing with a prominent member of the *ton.*

With Hamish being a marquess and the sole heir to the dukedom of Mildenwoode, Hamish certainly fit that bill!

As the carriage trundled ever closer to Beaumore Manor that evening, Hamish couldn't help but feel anxious about seeing his father again. Their argument over the proposed marriage of convenience between Hamish and Lady Josette had clouded the air between them. He had a feeling his father was not going to let it go so easily.

Hamish took in a deep breath. Fortunately, Beaumore Manor this evening was not the time for the duke to make a scene about it in public. At the very least, though, the Old Man would attempt to make him feel uncomfortable and try to get him alone outside the ballroom, perhaps in the gardens. All in an effort to get Hamish to agree that the duke's idea was best for his son's future.

Hamish strongly disagreed, never more so than that evening.

His heart skipped when the carriage finally arrived at the Beaumore Manor and he alighted. He breathed deeply and looked about him at the other arriving guests, though they hardly interested him. The night was about successfully presenting Miss Beaumont to the *ton*, and there was no reason for his problems to make the evening any harder for her. It was best to make sure she heard nothing about it.

He would make sure of that.

The drawing room of Beaumore Manor had probably not seen such activity since the wedding of Anthony and Bridget. Many prominent members of the *ton* had already arrived, and Hamish could hear nothing above the loud buzz of conversation going on. He was sure there were plenty of people speculating about Miss Beaumont and why her name had already appeared in the scandal sheets, with the writer claiming unkindly that she was 'too plain.'

Hamish wanted to set everyone straight and tell them that looks were not all that mattered, not that Miss Beaumont was at all plain. Quite the opposite, in his eyes. But he decided it would do him no favors. He had already gotten on the wrong side of his father, and most likely the Earl of Ashington too.

"Oh, Hamish! There you are, old lad, a pleasure to see you here!"

Anthony's voice came from nearby. Hamish turned to face his friend, glad for the warm welcome. He hoped for another just as warm from Miss Beaumont, but he noted she hadn't yet entered the room. He smiled to think that if she had, she would have been equally pleased to see him as Anthony had, if not more.

"Anthony, how lovely to be invited to this grand affair. I'm honored," he said, shaking Anthony's hand vigorously. "This is all absolutely splendid. Just splendid."

As they left him to mingle with the gathering crowd, Hamish managed to spot his parents off in the far corner of the drawing room. They were standing with the Ashmore family.

As much as it was going to pain him, he decided it would be best to attempt to talk to his family early on and get it over with. At least his mother would talk to him, even if his father was still furious at him for daring to oppose his wishes. It would be considered highly impolite not to talk to his parents while they were at the same function.

His stomach twisted as he approached them, hoping it would be easier to keep his father calm here, in front of everyone. The last thing he wanted was the duke's anger to ruin Miss Beaumont's coming out ball.

"Hamish, I'm glad to see you made it." His mother, at least, looked at him with a smile. "I hear Miss Beaumont is to arrive soon."

"A joy to see you, Mother," Hamish said, ignoring the last comment.

The duke, on the other hand, only nodded before completely ignoring him. Judging by the way his nostrils flared softly, it was clear to Hamish that his father was still angry at having lost control of his son while he'd been in the Far East and able to think for himself. Then again, Hamish thought, his father should not have been surprised.

He had done well in the Far East, deciding for himself what advice to listen to when it came time to make important decisions.

"Hello again, Lord Milington," Lady Josette said, fluttering her fan and her eyelashes at him. His heart sank as he turned to face them.

"I am glad to see you here," Lady Rosalie said, smiling at him sweetly.

"Ladies," he said, bowing. Holding his breath, he turned to the Earl and Countess of Ashington. Would they speak to him? But the earl simply nodded his head in greeting, and the countess puckered her lips as if in disapproval when acknowledging him.

If that was it, he was relieved. He was about to excuse himself when the countess cleared her throat and spoke.

"I hear Miss Beaumont has not yet shown her face because she is far too ugly to feel comfortable among such grand company," the Countess of Ashington said abruptly. "She has such a lackluster set of eyes, and hair like straw."

Both Lady Josette and Lady Rosalie smiled and muttered their agreement. Meanwhile, though he did his best to hide it, Hamish's anger rose inside him. How could they derive pleasure from spreading such vicious gossip?

And Lady Josette's eyelashes fluttering at him didn't escape his notice either. It incensed Hamish further when the duke even laughed a little at the Countess of Ashington's unkind comment about Miss Beaumont.

At least his mother had the good sense to know when it was not fitting to do so. She might not have gone against the duke at home, but she was willing to defend Miss Beaumont in public. Thankfully.

However, it was the way Lady Josette and her sister reacted to the comment that made Hamish all the more confused. How could his father possibly be oblivious to how horrid this whole family could be to anyone they didn't like? Could His Grace not see how insufferable it made the Ashmore family to the rest of the *ton*? And how it rubbed off on their own family name.

He wanted nothing to do with the worst gossips in Town, though he could see that the duke didn't seem to see their behavior that way. All His Grace saw was that the Earl of Ashington was a good businessman, but even that reputation was questionable as far as Hamish was concerned. He recalled the earl promising to arrange for him to see the account books for the

Ashmore's various business interests, but nothing had come of that so far.

His thoughts were interrupted by a sudden silence falling all around him. Thinking he might have drawn attention to himself somehow, he glanced around. Hamish was glad to see the silence was nothing to do with him, but instead because the doors of the drawing room had just opened.

Miss Beaumont stepped into the room, and Hamish could hardly believe it was the same woman he had met on the steps of Beaumore Manor all those weeks ago. Tonight, he thought she must be the most beautiful woman in the room, and certainly the most beautiful woman he had ever laid eyes on.

She wore an underskirt of ivory satin beneath a beautiful gown of white sarsenet. The light from the chandeliers caught on the pearls adorning the dress, arranged in delicate rosettes. Around her neck was a single strand of lustrous pearls, set off by elbow-length ivory silk gloves. Her hair had been done atop her head, with some light curls framing her face, and a small pearl tiara completed the look to perfection.

If he hadn't known any better, he would have thought her a princess in that moment. Despite her background, she looked every bit the elegant Society lady.

She greeted several guests as she made her way into the room, and Hamish could not stop watching her every move. Not to judge her, no, but to admire the graceful way she moved despite knowing that everyone else was sizing her up.

Eventually, she drew near to where he was standing. He looked towards his parents and the Ashmore family.

"If you'll excuse me, I have some business to attend to," Hamish said with a soft bow to everyone.

He met her halfway, calculating that it would allow his parents, and Lady Josette in particular, to see where his interests truly lay.

"Good evening, Miss Beaumont. Congratulations on a lovely ball. Might I just say you look lovely tonight?"

Hamish smiled as he bowed to her.

Miss Beaumont dipped an elegant curtsey in return, blushing and smiling at him as she straightened.

"Hello, Lord Milington. I am so glad you were able to come tonight."

Though her voice held steady, he knew her well enough to tell she was nervous. Her smile tilted sideways, but she held her poise regardless. Someone had given her lessons in making her face less expressive, which he was grateful for just then. With people like the Ashmore family present, she needed to be perfect.

But he was not going to mention that to her for fear of making her feel even more nervous.

"It will all be all right, Miss Beaumont," Hamish said quietly. "You are already impressing everyone. Be yourself. In my opinion, any lady who would rather spread vicious rumors than spend time getting to know you is ill-suited for High Society. And any man who would believe those rumors is unworthy of your company."

She giggled, relaxing a little. The sound charmed him.

"I have only been in the room but a few minutes," she confessed, "and I already wish to leave. Is that normal, Lord Milington?"

"Probably. For one's first ball, I'll wager many a young lady has felt the same," he replied, laughing. "But you will do wonderfully. All the hard work you have put in is already starting to show."

"How so?"

"If you had not said anything about it, I would have assumed you were merely being reserved with your feelings, holding everything back until after the ball. Many ladies are that way." He smiled. "Take heart, Miss Beaumont, for if I could not tell, then no one here should be able to, either."

She opened her mouth to say something but was interrupted by the announcement that dinner was ready.

Perfect timing, Hamish thought, extending his arm to Miss Beaumont before Lady Josette had a chance to grab him.

"Allow me to escort you into dinner, Miss Beaumont," he said, feeling a deep sense of satisfaction when she nodded and took his arm without hesitation, a small smile on her face.

As he started to walk her towards the dining room, Hamish didn't fail to spot the very pointed looks coming from his father and the Ashmores. He paid them no heed. There was someone else on his mind . . .

# Chapter Twenty-One

Her stomach dropped as the doors to the drawing room opened, and she would have been lying if she said she didn't feel intimidated. As she made her initial rounds of greeting the guests, Catriona could feel all the eyes in the room on her. *They're all waiting for me to make a mistake!* It wasn't until Lord Milington approached her that she felt able to relax somewhat.

It had been Bridget's idea to have Lord Milington stand close enough for him to offer her his arm and escort to the dining room after her entrance into the drawing room. Catriona was quite happy with the arrangement. If she'd had to be escorted by someone she didn't know, she wasn't sure if she could have managed it!

Her stomach settled a little as she put her hand on Lord Milington's arm to go into dinner. Somehow, just being around him always made things feel a lot easier. She didn't have to deal with the pressure of having to have perfect manners around him. Perhaps it was just because he had been able to see her transformation from the girl from the orphanage to the lady she was supposed to be that night. She knew he wouldn't judge her for a misstep. All she knew was that she was quite happy to have the extra help he offered and the way he relaxed her without even meaning to.

Once in the dining room, Catriona remembered with a silent sigh of relief that she was seated between Lord Milington and Bridget for dinner. She needn't be utterly perfect during the meal. Lady Spencer had suggested seating the two people who made her feel most at ease next to her, which was partially what had inspired Bridget to arrange for Lord Milington to be Catriona's escort that night.

She had a feeling Lady Spencer sensed a connection between her and Lord Milington, perhaps even suspecting he was enamored of her niece and might eventually want to court her after the ball. Catriona would not have been surprised if her aunt was right. There was nothing she wanted more . . .

Her thoughts were interrupted by Anthony tapping on his glass, calling for the guests' attention. She looked over to him, happy for a few moments at least, that the spotlight would not be on her.

He raised his glass as the rest of the guests looked towards him.

"I propose a toast, to Miss Catriona Beaumont. May the newest member of the *ton* always feel welcome among us. To Miss Beaumont, everyone!"

Catriona smiled shyly at the rest of the guests as they echoed the toast and turned in her direction to drink her health. She hid her terror behind her glass as she took a sip of the wine.

Then, the conversation returned to normal. While she might have been sitting between Lord Milington and Bridget, across the table from her was Lady Josette Ashmore. Catriona noticed that the young lady had been glaring at her ever since they had all sat down, only daring to look away when she was afraid she would be caught.

The glare was angry, and Catriona wondered again how she had earned Lady Josette's dislike? Why had the woman been seated across from her? It made Catriona feel very uncomfortable.

As dinner was served, Catriona tried to put her concerns about Lady Josette aside. She told herself that there was no reason to worry about being stared at that evening—it was to be expected. She was honestly more worried about spilling something on her white dress and making a fool of herself in front of everyone.

She could hardly bring herself to eat, though she took a few small bites of everything on her plate to be sure she had something in her stomach for later.

"Are you feeling well, Miss Beaumont?"

Lord Milington's whisper caught her attention. She turned to face him.

"I'm anxious about having to open the dance floor later tonight, Lord Milington," she confessed, taking in a deep breath.

After having shared something of her experiences in the orphanage with him, he probably knew why it had her so worried. Everything had to be done *just so*. And if she didn't do it right, more unkind rumors would circulate and ruin her reputation before it had even started.

"You have nothing to worry about," he said with a soft smile. "Just remember to block out your surroundings. Whoever your partner is on the floor, imagine you are the only two in the room. If you remember that, then I am sure you will be just fine. You always were when we danced together."

She managed a smile, though she could feel an intense glare coming from across the table.

"Thank you, Lord Milington."

He nodded at her and returned to his food. Catriona moved just slightly in her seat to do the same, and now she caught sight of Lady Josette again. The woman had moved from glaring at Catriona to attempting to get Lord Milington's attention without outright waving to him. It was rather sad to watch as Lady Josette ignored the man who had escorted her into the dining room and fixed her eyes on the man who hardly seemed to notice her.

After Lord Milington's perfect reassurances, Catriona was able to actually eat. And she put his tip to good use at the dinner table, pretending that Lady Josette was smiling instead of glaring at her. While she may not have been able to entirely forget that Lady Josette disliked her for some reason, she knew Lord Milington's advice would be enough to keep her going for the evening.

At the end of dinner, Bridget stood up with Anthony. It was the announcement that Catriona had been dreading all evening; the dance floor was officially open in the ballroom, and it was time for the party to really begin.

Lord Milington escorted her to the ballroom with a knowing glance. It was going to be all right so long as she remembered his advice. The music would play, and she could let her partner lead her around the floor with no difficulty.

Once in the ballroom, Lady Spencer took her aside as the orchestra began the interlude. People hurried to find a partner and began getting into position on the floor for the first dance.

"For this evening to be a success, Catriona," Lady Spencer said, "you must make no mistakes while dancing."

Catriona felt her stomach drop at the reminder, but she nodded.

"I will give it my best, Lady Spencer." She managed a smile.

With that, Lady Spencer excused herself. Catriona moved towards the dance floor, knowing Anthony would find her to ask her for the first dance. She had specifically requested that her first dance of the night be with someone she knew.

"May I have this dance, Miss Beaumont?" Anthony's voice came as expected, and she smiled more brightly.

"Yes, you may, Viscount Beaumore."

With that, she took his arm.

He led her onto the floor for the first dance set, and she took in a deep breath. She had danced with him before, and honestly, it had not been the worst thing in the world. He at least understood the reason for her tension—all eyes were upon them.

However, the music for their set began, and she adopted Lord Milington's advice at once. As Anthony led her around the ballroom, she kept her gaze locked on him and pretended they were the only two on the floor.

"You're doing well, Catriona. Something tells me tonight is going to go well, I can see it," Anthony mused as they danced. "Just keep it up while you're on the floor for the rest of the night. I know that sounds like a long time, but it's not as hard as it sounds. You might even come to enjoy it."

"Thank you for that, Anthony," she said, doubt in her voice. "I appreciate the enthusiasm you have for this to be a success. I think we all want that."

Just then, the music ended. It hadn't been a long conversation, but it had been enough for her to know that Anthony was among those rooting for her success tonight. That was enough for her to consider the first dance a success. Plus, she was also quite proud that she had not trampled on his feet excessively. Or at all . . . but then, if she had, Anthony would not have said a word about it.

As Anthony returned to Bridget's side, a few guests she didn't know approached her. She summoned a wide smile to appear, though smiling was the last thing she felt like doing. Her cheeks were going to be sore by the end of the night, she was sure!

"Congratulations," one said.

"Welcome," another said.

The theme continued, and she was relieved to find that everyone who approached her either complimented her on a dance well done or welcomed her into High Society. It was rather overwhelming at first, and she noticed a group who did not come to welcome her—Lady Henrietta Ashmore and her daughters. They were conspicuously absent from the crowd fawning over her and how well she was doing.

Was it a purposeful snub, or had they not been able to find her in time before she had been surrounded by the rest of the guests? Perhaps they were waiting to offer her their felicitations later.

She took in a deep breath and focused her attention instead on the men and women congratulating her.

The party continued in that manner until the orchestra struck up the first chords of a waltz, indicating that the dancers should make ready.

Her stomach started to flutter when she realized Lord Milington had begun to walk her way. He had been in conversation with Anthony and Bridget. Catriona watched in horror as Lady Josette moved deliberately in front of him, batting her eyelashes. But her heart soared when he politely excused himself and continued walking towards her.

She didn't see the aftermath of the dismissal, as Lord Milington's body now blocked her view of Lady Josette. However, she didn't really care what the woman thought. Her thoughts were all for Lord Milington, who, as far as she was concerned, was the picture of a well-bred gentleman.

"May I have this dance, Miss Beaumont?"

"Of course, you may, Lord Milington," Catriona said smiling as she took his arm.

# Chapter Twenty-Two

Hamish felt the thrill of his feelings for Miss Beaumont coursing hotly through his body as he led her onto the dance floor for the waltz. They got into position on the floor, and as he put his hand on her lower back for proper frame, he couldn't help but feel the electric connection between them again.

Then, the music began properly, and he began to lead her across the floor. She appeared to have taken his advice to heart, as he was able to spin her through even the most difficult of steps easily. It was actually quite fun, and he had to admit she had come far since the first dance he had shared with her at that small dinner party.

"No one will be able to fault you for anything that happens tonight," Hamish whispered to her. "You are the picture of a perfect lady tonight, and I must say that I am quite pleased to know that you will dance with me regardless of who is watching."

"You make it easy to dance," she replied in the same hushed tone. "Thank you for being so kind . . . and encouraging. I've needed it this week."

She gave him a soft smile as they continued to twirl around the ballroom.

However, he didn't fail to spot the way Lady Josette Ashmore was staring at him from across the ballroom and across her partner's shoulders. In that moment, he could not have cared less, though he realized it was a look of intense jealousy.

He shrugged it off. She could be as jealous as she liked. He would rather go to war than marry Lady Josette, and the way she had been behaving this evening only further cemented that resolution in his head. She had almost taken hold of his arm before he had been able to ask Miss Beaumont about escorting her into dinner. Then, she had actually stood in front of him and attempted to make conversation when he was on his way to ask Miss Beaumont to dance the waltz with him.

But how could such a beautiful woman be so jealous of a woman so 'plain' as Miss Beaumont? He knew it had been the Ashmores who had deliberately spread that lie about Catriona, no doubt as vengeance for the attention Hamish had shown her in the park. Lady Josette had no clue that she was showing him every moment why she was the kind of woman he would rather die than marry. The whole family's spiteful behavior simply made them appear . . . what was the right word for it?

Covetous, he supposed, would be the best word. Lady Josette certainly wanted him to look at her the way he was looking at Miss Beaumont just then. But then again, what single young lady wouldn't want him to pay attention to them? He was, after all, the sole heir to the dukedom of Mildenwoode.

Though, he had a feeling it might not remain that way for much longer if he didn't marry Lady Josette. He supposed it was better to have a woman who entirely understood the implications of what their courtship could mean for Hamish's future than to have a woman who would rather get the man she wanted at the expense of his happiness— and perhaps even her own.

He wondered if Lady Josette had even considered how happy *she* would be in a marriage with him. If he couldn't stand to be around her, would she be happy with that, or would she take lovers?

He shook the thoughts away. This was not the time nor the place to be thinking about what kind of relationship he might have with Lady Josette if he were to actually marry her. For now, the attention was to be entirely on Miss Beaumont.

Thankfully, she had not seemed to notice his distraction. Hamish gave himself over to the wonderful feeling of holding her in his arms and gazing down into her beautiful blue eyes.

The waltz eventually ended, and Hamish couldn't help but feel disappointed. He wanted to keep dancing with Miss Beaumont, but, unfortunately, there was no more music. Reluctantly. he escorted her back to where her family stood waiting for her.

He was quite glad to see the dowager viscountess beaming at Miss Beaumont as they arrived.

"You were nothing less than the absolute *depiction* of elegance and grace out there, Catriona," the Dowager Viscountess Beaumont said. "What a lovely first dance. Absolutely lovely. And you, Lord Milington, thank you for helping Catriona to do such a beautiful job on the floor."

Hamish offered a smile.

"It was my pleasure, my lady. Now, if you would all excuse me," he said, bowing, as he wished to have a word with Anthony, who was standing nearby with Bridget.

With that, Miss Beaumont let go of his arm, and he approached Anthony and Bridget, who had made their little camp in on the sidelines of the dancefloor.

"Hamish, you were brilliant on the dance floor," Anthony said. "Brilliant, just brilliant. But . . . I couldn't help but notice you seemed a little preoccupied. What's wrong?"

"Lady Josette is struggling with the idea that the world does not revolve around her," Hamish said carefully. "I fear I'm going to have to dance with her tonight at some point."

Anthony snickered.

"If you don't want to dance with her, it will not be a snub. You two aren't courting, and no one else knows what your father is expecting of you. But you didn't hear that from me."

Hamish smiled.

"Thank you, Anthony."

The night went smoothly enough. The dance floor finally closed in the early hours, and Hamish was happy to find himself dancing the final set with Miss Beaumont. After that, she and the ladies retired to the drawing room for refreshments and conversation.

Hamish walked with the other men into the parlor for drinks. He wished Miss Beaumont could have been with him to make his point, as he knew this was when he was going to have to face his father alone.

"Hamish . . . may I have a word with you?"

The duke approached him at that very moment, and Hamish only nodded. His stomach dropped like a rock as he walked with his father into a far corner of the parlor. He well knew there was only one reason for the privacy, His Grace had something important to say, though he hadn't spoken a word to his son all evening. What would he make of Hamish dancing with Miss Beaumont twice, opening the ball with her, and dancing a waltz?

Hamish watched as his father's expression turned stern the moment they were out of earshot.

"I know now why you've been stalling on settling your marriage to Lady Josette," the duke said. The stern expression turned into a sneer as he continued. "It's rather obvious that you fancy the poor orphan girl who is now Miss Beaumont."

"And what if I do prefer her?" Hamish did not immediately own up to it. He wanted to see what his father would say about Miss Beaumont first, though if he knew His Grace, he would behave much like the Ashmores and despise her for getting in the way of their 'perfect' union between Hamish and Josette.

"You'd better think very carefully about your future, as I will have no problem cutting off your allowance if you wish to pursue Miss Beaumont. She is not the sort of lady suitable for a man of your stature to marry. You are indeed quite lucky that Lady Henrietta has kept her eldest daughter occupied for the night. It would be a devastating blow to Miss Beaumont's reputation if she were to have such a prominent lady of the *ton* start accusing her in public of coming between her and her fiancé, after all."

Hamish had no time to respond before His Grace walked away to join the Earl of Ashington at another table nearby. He had a feeling that his father had intentionally led him that way so the earl could hear him rebuke him for not paying court to Lady Josette in favor of Miss Beaumont.

He simply curled his fingers into a fist as he counted to ten. This was not the time nor the place to get angry about the duke attempting to use the rules of propriety against him. It had been something he had entirely expected upon his return from the Far East.

What he hadn't expected was that his father was just as willing to ruin a woman's reputation just because she was coming between him and a business deal. Hamish felt he might have seen such a move coming from the Earl of Ashington—he already had a reputation for being a rather unscrupulous man—but from his own father?

And to threaten his allowance at that?

He walked away to join Anthony and a few other younger men at another table, where they were drinking port and enjoying some light conversation.

However, Anthony soon noticed something was amiss with his friend. Instead of approaching Hamish about it, Anthony simply gave him a glass of port, a silent suggestion to drink and forget whatever it was until the morrow.

Hamish took the glass gladly. He was not going to put the ball in jeopardy. And for now, it seemed he had escaped making the Ashmores more angry at how he was treating Miss Beaumont instead of showing his favor to Lady Josette. Miss Beaumont's happiness was his main concern.

At the end of the night, Hamish left without saying goodbye to his father. Well, perhaps the more accurate statement was that his father had left the party early and not bothered to say goodbye to Hamish.

As far as Hamish was concerned, so long as the Ashmores had not tried anything to sabotage Miss Beaumont's ball, he was sure it would be deemed a great success and a good thing for her growing reputation.

"I look forward to seeing how the press handles the coverage of the ball tonight, Anthony," Hamish said as he walked out with his friend. "Beaumore Manor has not seen a party of this caliber since your wedding, and I would like to think it has helped the *ton* to accept Miss Beaumont more fully into their midst."

"Me too, Hamish. Thank you for not making a scene with your father or Lady Josette tonight," Anthony said. "I could tell they were doing their best to cause something to happen between Lady Josette and Catriona, or perhaps between you and Catriona, but it didn't work."

"I paid them no heed until the very end," he said. "I was afraid my father or the Earl of Ashington would find a way to cause a scene if they were left alone. I am glad I managed to avoid them until the end."

"I'll see you soon, then, Hamish," Anthony said. "Have a good ride home."

"Thank you."

With that, Hamish was soon in his carriage on the way home, musing on what a success the ball had been for Miss Beaumont.

## Chapter Twenty-Three

*Knock, knock, knock.*

The faint sounds of knocking woke Catriona up from a sweet dream of waltzing with Lord Milington. She felt there hadn't been nearly enough waltzes played the night before at the ball. But she admitted to herself that she was probably so partial to the dance because of her partner. Lord Milington had made sure to ask her for both waltz sets, and she was in seventh heaven over it.

When Alice arrived, she had the latest editions of the scandal sheets in her hand.

"Morning, dear friend," Alice said as she moved rapidly toward the bed. "You need to see this, now!"

"Oh?" Catriona woke up quickly as her heart began to race in her chest.

"The *ton* reports that Miss . . ."

"Oh-oh, slow down, Alice! Give me that paper," Catriona said, laughing, half in fear, half in excitement.

"No, no, let me read it, please," Alice pleaded, keeping the sheet and continued reading, more slowly this time.

"The *ton* reports that Miss Beaumont handled herself with the utmost elegance and grace last night," Catriona read aloud from the paper. "Her ball was a splendid affair, and though there was indeed some worry she would not be up to the task beforehand, it is perfectly clear that the beautiful Miss Beaumont is every inch her father's daughter."

Catriona grinned with relief as she looked up at Alice.

"I know. Isn't it wonderful!?" Alice grinned back.

Catriona's long held back emotions came pouring out, tears of relief, of happiness, and of satisfaction that she had pulled it off against all the odds.

Alice pulled Catriona into a sisterly embrace.

"I'm so proud of you, Catriona. That ball must have been more exhausting than I could ever imagine, and after all that preparation too," Alice said, releasing her. "Now, you have done it, so you can relax a little. But now, I must help you dress for breakfast, so come on, get up."

Catriona obeyed, her heart light for the first time in many weeks. She read over the scandal sheets again as Alice helped her out of her night clothes, into a new morning dress, and arranged her hair in a simple bun.

"I feel quite the proper lady," she joked as they set off down the hall toward the dining room. She paused outside the door. Last night had been the moment everyone had been waiting for, the moment she had trained so hard for. To know that the presentation was finally over and that her family was about to cast a judgment on her was freshly overwhelming for her. What if the others didn't think much of the review of her ball?

She forced herself to relax, to push those thoughts from her mind. There was nothing more she wanted just then than to see her family happy for her and happy with their work. She hoped that even Lady Spencer would be pleased to see that there was hope for her yet in High Society. Especially Lady Spencer. Would she ever understand her aunt?

Catriona stepped into the dining room. Everyone was standing, talking. They turned to her as one before Eleanor moved forward and pulled Catriona into a warm embrace. It startled the young woman, as she had never seen Eleanor embrace anyone except Lady Spencer and Mrs. Mills.

Catriona put her arms around the older woman as she returned the hug.

"You have made me an extremely proud grandmother," Eleanor said, pulling away slightly so Catriona could see the wide smile on her face. "You handled everything last night with such poise, such grace. Truly, I believe Chilton would have been proud to see it too. And I must admit to being quite upset that he waited until he was dying to give us the gift of having you in our family."

"I never thought you would be able to pull everything off in such a short time, Catriona," Lady Spencer said with a smile, "but you have made the entire Beaumont family proud."

Catriona grinned, quite overcome with happiness.

All the fears that had taken over her thoughts in the hallway were instantly put to rest as the rest of the family offered their own congratulations. There was much excited chatter about how well the ball had gone. It seemed, for now, that she was the only one who had noticed how Lady Josette Ashmore had glared at her the entire night.

Or she was the only one who seemed to care. She made a note to herself to talk to Bridget about it as soon as they were alone. In the meantime, her appetite had returned, and she set about getting some breakfast.

Shortly after Catriona sat down to start eating, Anthony called for everyone's attention.

"I propose a toast in Catriona's honor," he said. "You had a hard life, no one here can deny that, before you came to us. And we all had to admit to ourselves that there was something about you that stood out when you first arrived at Beaumore Manor. To say you have surprised us all by becoming a lady in such a short time is an understatement. To say that it is nothing short of a miracle might be more accurate, knowing how harsh the *ton* can be. Here's to you, Catriona, the woman who can make anything possible."

It took all of Catriona's will not to start sobbing right there as the rest of the family raised their glasses to join in the toast. Catriona took her glass and raised it high. She had done something amazing, something that she had doubted she was capable of.

With breakfast over and the various family members eventually taking their leave, Catriona managed to catch Bridget alone.

"Bridget, if you have a moment . . .there is something about last night that has been worrying me. I would like to talk to you about it."

"I caught how Lady Josette was looking at you, too, if that's what has you so worried," Bridget said. "The Ashmore family, while incredible gossips, would never try to destroy anyone's reputation because of simple jealousy, I'm certain. But you might be right to worry. For now, nothing has come of it in the scandal sheets, and unless she actually confronts you over it, I do not believe you have any reason to worry."

"I'm more worried she shall try to confront Lord Milington," Catriona confessed.

"Oh, you need not worry about Lord Milington if she tries that," Bridget said with a laugh. "He has been through the wringer and back with the scandal sheets and come out the better for it. I doubt he would think twice of setting the record straight before anything became of it. There is a reason Anthony trusted him to be in the manor before you were officially presented to the *ton*."

"And that reason is?"

"Lord Milington and Anthony grew up together," Bridget said. "If he couldn't trust you around Lord Milington before you were a lady, then the problem would not have been with you. It would have been with Lord Milington, as you originally had no idea how to act in his presence."

Catriona nodded slowly.

"Thank you."

"Of course. I didn't think anything of having Lord Milington escort you to dinner until I saw the way Lady Josette was looking at you across the table and her glaring attempts to get Lord Milington to notice her." Bridget shook her head. "A proper lady would have understood that Anthony and Lord Milington are friends, and as such, he was probably one of the few people you knew at the ball."

With Catriona's nerves calmed, she and Bridget parted ways. As Catriona headed towards the ballroom, perhaps to relive some of the best memories from the night before—her waltzes with Lord Milington the high points—the butler announced there was a gentleman come to call on her and was waiting in the drawing room. She sent the butler to fetch Bridget before doing anything.

With Bridget by her side, she entered the drawing room.

Over the course of the morning, several gentlemen she had met at the ball had called on her. Thankfully, Bridget was understanding and acted as chaperone, working on her needlepoint and guiding the conversation for the entire morning.

Each gentleman had come with a bouquet of flowers for Catriona, congratulating her on her lovely ball and complimenting her appearance. Each was introduced with a title, and though they were all quite handsome and polite . . . she couldn't help but wish Lord Milington would call on her instead.

As one of the gentlemen left, another large bouquet now set on the table, Catriona turned to Bridget.

"Is it normal for so many gentlemen to come calling on a woman after she has been presented to the *ton*?"

"Yes, it is," Bridget said, now looking up from what she had been working on. "I remember that after my presentation, I was met by several suitors calling upon me that week. Anthony was one of them, though it took me a while to remember he'd called and finally accept he was actually interested in me and not merely visiting out of politeness."

"They do that? Simply visit out of politeness instead of a wish to get to know a woman better?" Catriona raised an eyebrow.

"Oh, especially when the woman in question may not know exactly how High Society works," Bridget cautioned. "Though several of your callers are men known for having a good reputation, I would not be surprised to learn that one of them is hiding some other motive for wanting to get to know you. With your last name comes the knowledge that you are an heiress to a fortune."

Catriona nodded.

"Do you believe Lord Milington will call on me today?"

"Oh, Catriona, I'd be surprised if it took him longer than two days to do so," Bridget said with a laugh. "If I had to guess, I believe he has quite enjoyed your company in the time that you've gotten to know him, in between all the preparations for your ball. If he were not to come over specifically to seek you out, I would be quite shocked."

Hearing Bridget would also be shocked to know if Lord Milington only called at the manor for business and not to specifically see Catriona made her feel better. She just wanted him to call on her officially, like the rest of gentlemen that morning.

He didn't even have to bring flowers for her. All he had to do was come, and she would consider it a great success.

There were more gentlemen callers before the conversation between Catriona and Bridget could continue. Bridget usually stayed silent, letting Catriona handle her visitors herself. She was glad it was Bridget who was chaperoning the visits. Lady Spencer might have considered none of the gentlemen as good enough for Catriona and sent them packing. The thought made Catriona chuckle to herself.

And every time the butler announced a new visitor, she prayed it was Lord Milington. However, as the morning drew to a close now, he still had not appeared. She wondered what could be keeping him from calling on her, or if he simply had a list of things he had to do first.

Bridget eventually had to leave her, so Alice was called in to chaperone the afternoon visitors.

# Chapter Twenty-Four

The next morning, Hamish could hardly believe the conversation with the duke at Miss Beaumont's ball had really happened. How could His Grace threaten to cut off his allowance for simply wanting to be happy in his marriage? At this point, it wasn't even about finding love in marriage anymore. It was about Hamish's wish to marry someone who's company he enjoyed, which clashed with His Grace's insistence that a marriage of convenience for personal gain was the only *correct* way to approach it.

As far as Hamish was concerned, his father could do as he pleased in an attempt to enforce his will. Over the years, Hamish had been able to make some wise investments. There was also the business venture with Anthony that he was in the process of finalizing.

There was no need for him to rely on the duke's money any longer. He would be independent.

The only question he had was whether or not His Grace would actually go through with it. He knew his father would always want to remain the person Hamish went to for advice, but Hamish wanted him to understand that he could not be controlled by threats of being cut off. The money no longer meant anything to him.

If the duke had thought he would be able to control his son while Hamish was in the Far East, he had soon learned he was very wrong indeed. Hamish would never agree to marry Lady Josette.

To Hamish, his choice was clear.

He rose from the couch and readied himself for the day with the help of his valet. The family money meant nothing to him if it gave the duke a way to rule over him. And his father had no right to demand so much of him.

In the carriage on the way to Beaumore Manor, Hamish knew only one thing: if his business deal with Anthony was finalized today, then there was really no reason to delay asking for permission to court Miss Beaumont. He would, of course, want Anthony's blessing.

It was odd to think that Anthony was the head of the Beaumont family now . . . but then again, that had happened while Hamish was in the Far East.

If he were honest, now Miss Beaumont was in the picture, he was quite glad the title and related duties fell to Anthony.

The carriage arrived at the manor and stopped in the drive. But that is not what caught Hamish's attention when he alighted. That was the large number of gentlemen coming and going from the manor. Whatever was the reason for so many gentlemen to be calling?

"I shall escort you to his lordship's office, my lord. He is expecting you," the butler told him.

Hamish couldn't help but smile. It seemed Anthony shared his enthusiasm for their shared business venture. This was going to be their last meeting before things were wrapped up, and they were to sign the papers to finalize it that day.

That was very good indeed.

Leonard escorted Hamish to Anthony's office, where he then knocked on the door. Anthony opened it with a wide smile.

"It's wonderful to see you, Hamish. Did you have any trouble getting past the gentlemen all vying for Catriona's attention this morning?" Anthony asked off-handedly as he turned back towards the desk.

Hamish gulped hard, his stomach knotting. Those gentlemen were here for Catriona, not to help Bridget with a surprise for Anthony? How dare they?

Then, with horror, he realized that the rush of burning fury coursing through him must have been much like that which Lady Josette had felt the night before when she had seen him dancing the waltz with Miss Beaumont. Jealousy! Jealous of everyone else in the room who was receiving his attention. He almost felt sorry for her. Almost.

At least Hamish had the good grace to try to hide his emotions in the moment.

What he couldn't hide, at least to himself, was how strongly he felt about Miss Beaumont. He had developed much stronger feelings for her than he had realized. Why else would he be feeling jealous at the mere mention of other gentlemen vying for her attention? There hadn't even been any mention of her *wanting* that attention, or of any of those gentlemen approaching Anthony for permission to court Miss Beaumont.

"You'll have to excuse me for changing our original plans for our discussion, Anthony," Hamish said simply, "but there have been a few things that have come up which I would like your advice on . . . and a question I think you'll have the answer to."

"Then, please, ask away." Anthony sat down behind his desk, motioning for Hamish to do the same. "I have all morning."

"Well, I am sure you remember how I looked yesterday when I sat down to have drinks and speak with you and some of our other friends in the parlor," Hamish began. "I had just spoken to my father at that point. He threatened to cut my allowance off if I do not marry Lady Josette Ashmore."

"I'm sorry, Hamish," Anthony said with a frown. "That's a rough thing to hear. What do you plan to do?"

"Well, hearing just now that there are gentlemen here vying for Miss Beaumont's attention has crystallized my decision. My father can cut my allowance off if he wishes, for I have no wish to marry Lady Josette," Hamish responded. "I actually . . . I would like your permission to court Miss Beaumont. Anthony, I would be lying if I didn't tell you that I felt such a surge of jealousy just now, upon hearing that all these visitors are for her. I do not wish to do things in a manner that will affect her reputation adversely, not after all the work you've put in to make sure she has a reputation to begin with . . ."

Hamish sighed and ran a hand through his hair.

Anthony leaned back for a moment.

"And you feel so strongly that you have decided to ask for my permission to court her instead of finalizing the business deal today?"

"If you need time to think, I would be more than happy to finalize that deal here and now," Hamish replied. "I feel so strongly, I can no longer delay acting on my feelings for Miss Beaumont. There is no harm in at least asking, is there?" he finished, impatient for an answer.

Anthony pulled a pen and inkwell from the side of the desk and handed it to Hamish. Without a second thought, he took the pen and signed the forms.

"I know this was what we originally meant to do today, and I apologize. But some things must take precedence . . . Once I heard there were other gentlemen vying for the attention of Miss Beaumont, I had to act."

"I wasn't sure you had made the connection when you came in so calmly," Anthony admitted with a smile. "Hamish, you are perhaps the only gentleman of the *ton* whom I trust with Catriona's reputation. She has had such a time putting it all together, and I do believe that having someone like you at her side through the first few months helped tremendously. You have my permission to court her, of course."

Hamish let go a huge sigh of relief and grinned as he watched Anthony sign the papers himself.

"And with that, not only do you have my permission to court her, but our deal is finalized. Would you like a drink to celebrate, or do you have something else in mind?"

Anthony's gaze met Hamish's, and he knew there was only one thing he wanted to do to celebrate their joint venture and the fact that Anthony had given him full permission to court Miss Beaumont.

"I do believe I shall go to the drawing room to call upon Miss Beaumont and pose the question of courtship to her," Hamish said as he stood up. "I do appreciate the fact that you were willing to mix business with my pleasure."

"Of course, Hamish. Of course," Anthony said. "Now . . . go and tell Catriona how you feel."

Hamish only smiled widely at that, his heart flying like a kite as he left the room and made his way to the drawing room.

Upon seeing Catriona, his heart thudded in his chest as she smiled at him. Her blonde hair had been pulled into a bun today, and her pale-blue eyes dazzled amid all of the flowers surrounding her. She wore a lilac dress this morning, which did nothing but show off the beauty of her complexion and the striking difference between the purple of the dress and the blue hue of her eyes in the early afternoon sunlight streaming through the windows.

Off in one of the corners, Miss Brown was reading a book. Most likely the chaperone for the day, her ears ready in case anything was said which could be deemed improper.

"Lord Milington . . . what a pleasure it is to see you again so soon," Miss Beaumont said, radiant. "I'm glad to see you were able to call on me this afternoon."

"I must admit I meant to get here earlier, but I had business to attend to with Anthony that had to be overseen first," he said. "I'm glad to see you'll have me as a visitor."

He took a seat on one of the chairs in the drawing room, and Miss Beaumont sat on the couch.

"Miss Beaumont . . . I feel we have got to know one another quite well over these last few weeks, and . . . I hope you don't think me too forward . . ." She beamed at him, which encouraged him onward. "Well, nothing would make me happier than if you would . . . do me the honor of courting me." Hamish said, noticing the charming way her face had lit up. "You see, I came here with a singular goal in mind today, but seeing all of the gentlemen coming this morning to visit you has made me realize just how I feel about you. I became worried that if I did not declare myself at once, I might lose the chance for good."

"I-I . . . yes, I would be honored to court you, Lord Milington," Miss Beaumont gasped softly, tears shining in her eyes. She looked over at Miss Brown, who nodded encouragingly. They clearly shared a special bond, and he was glad someone was on hand to offer Miss Beaumont the comfort she might need in the moment.

"Then, I look forward to doing it properly very soon, then, Miss Beaumont."

Hamish stood up and gave a deep bow to Miss Beaumont. She rose to curtsey as he excused himself from the drawing room, with a promise to call upon her the following day as soon as he was free.

As he walked out of the drawing room, he could hear Miss Beaumont and Miss Brown both talking excitedly. Beyond the obvious excitement that came from his offer to court Miss Beaumont, he did not catch the topic of conversation.

Of course, he had decided not to tell Miss Beaumont that courting her would be going against his father's wishes. She didn't need to feel the pressure that would inevitably come with that, the wish to prove his father wrong. Hamish already felt it enough.

If he could protect Miss Beaumont from his father's controlling, callous ways for a little while longer as they began their courtship, he would happily do so. He just hoped she would allow that secret to remain his until he was ready to tell her.

# Chapter Twenty-Five

It was not but twenty-four hours later that Catriona sat on her bed, thoughts consumed with the fact that she was officially courting Lord Milington. It was going to be a beautiful courtship, she knew it. Everything had been going so well as of late . . . and she wanted absolutely nothing to ruin it for her. If she could only keep everything on course. With the help of her family, Catriona knew that at least her reputation would be safe.

Breakfast went well, with everyone congratulating Catriona on the courtship between herself and Lord Milington. Catriona could hardly eat because her stomach was so knotted up. He was to call on her later that day, but she had no idea when it would be.

It was shortly after breakfast that Bridget approached her as Catriona sat in the drawing room with a book in her hands. She'd finally had a chance to take Lord Milington's advice and found time to visit a circulating library the day before with Alice, when her gentleman callers had ceased their activities for the day.

"I hate to come between you and a good book," Bridget started, "but we have been invited to attend a soirée hosted by the Dowager Countess of Wesington tomorrow evening."

"The Dowager Countess of Wesington . . . I am not familiar with her." Catriona pursed her lips. "Was she at my ball the other night?"

"Yes, she was. She's known for throwing lavish social events," Bridget said. "If she's invited you, it's because either she wishes to see how you will do at an event where you are but a guest and not the main attraction, or she has decided that she simply wishes to get to know you better. Either way, to be invited to one of her parties is a mark of being accepted into High Society. Only the most prominent members of the *ton* are invited."

"Does that mean Lord Milington has received an invitation?"

"Oh, most certainly," Bridget said with a twinkle in her eyes. "It would be silly not to invite him when he is, as far as anyone else is concerned, a man of eligible status."

Catriona nodded.

"Well, I will have to be sure to find a proper dress in my wardrobe. Perhaps you could help me?"

"Of course, Catriona."

With that, Bridget smiled and went off to run some errands. Left alone again, Catriona's stomach churned. More parties, soirées, and social events were going to be coming her way, especially now she had been successfully presented and accepted into High Society.

She wasn't entirely sure she was ready for all of that . . . but she quietly resolved that she must at least *try* before she could say it wasn't for her. That, and it was entirely impolite to refuse an invitation when she was in perfect health.

Catriona ended up spending the morning in the drawing room, her head buried in a book. For just a day, she was able to relive the best moments of her early life and pretend she was anywhere but London for a few hours.

It all came to an end just before dinner. She had finished her book and fell to wondering if she had time to exchange it for a new one before the soirée tomorrow. Having someone else pick a book wouldn't work unless it was Alice who went, but Alice was busy, and Catriona feared her friend wouldn't have time either.

Now she had officially started courting Lord Milington.

That evening, Alice helped her into an evening dress. Lord Milington had finally called for her, as he had promised. They were to go for a ride along Rotten Row. Her evening dress was light-green, which emphasized her blue eyes beautifully.

As she walked down the hallway to make her way towards the staircase, Catriona felt her heart thudding in her chest. The realization hit her that this would be the first outing she and Lord Milington would have as a proper couple, courting in public. Was it normal for High Society couples to be seen in public so soon after they had started courting privately?

Her fears lessened the moment she saw Lord Milington standing in the hallway downstairs. He gave her a bow as she smiled at him.

"You look beautiful this evening, Miss Beaumont," he said as he extended his arm to her. "Shall we head to Rotten Row?"

"I would love to see Rotten Row, yes," Catriona said as she took his arm.

As they headed towards his carriage, she was very happy to know that Alice would be acting as their chaperone. Alice would certainly know how to tell Catriona if something was improper or impolite, but in a way that would not be embarrassing in public. For that reason, the only people Catriona trusted to properly chaperone her and Lord Milington were either Alice or Bridget.

The ride was quite lovely, and the spring day called to Catriona. It was beautiful outside. Why shouldn't they to take a walk in Hyde Park, after all? It would be an absolutely wonderful way to end the evening, in her mind.

"Why don't we go for a walk in Hyde Park?" She smiled as she made this suggestion. "It might help you feel less preoccupied."

"I believe you're right. A good walk in the park is always good for settling one's mind . . ."

Lord Milington's voice gave away that he was far more distracted than she had originally supposed him to be. He had been very quiet in the carriage.

They got out of the carriage at the park and started to take a slow stroll along the broad paths. Alice followed close behind. Catriona decided not to dwell too much on why Lord Milington was preoccupied. There were a thousand possibilities, and though the one that immediately came to mind was that he was nervous about their courtship, she knew she might be wrong. She hoped he would tell her in his own time.

"It's a beautiful day for a walk, Miss Beaumont," Lord Milington said. "Thank you for the suggestion. I fear I might have allowed it to go right past us without so much as a second thought if you had not said anything."

Catriona smiled.

"I wouldn't like you to miss out on this beauty, my lord," she said, gesturing to the greenery all around them.

They had just reached the end of a walkway when three ladies crossed their path. Catriona's heart sank; it was Lady Henrietta, Lady Josette, and Lady Rosalie Ashmore.

"Good evening, ladies," Lord Milington said with cool politeness, doffing his hat and bowing.

"Good evening, Lord Milington, Miss Beaumont," Lady Henrietta said.

"Good evening," Lady Josette said between gritted teeth.

"Good evening," Catriona replied, bobbing a small curtsey.

Lady Rosalie only smiled and returned the curtsey. While this might have passed with people who were not so attentive, Catriona could tell that the three women were completely insincere in their greetings. Their polite smiles were false.

In particular, she felt the heat of Lady Josette's displeasure. Catriona couldn't fail to spot the way Lady Josette stared at Lord Milington, the look in her eyes a mix of curiosity and jealousy. There was also an expectant air surrounding all three Ashmore ladies which made Catriona feel deeply unsettled.

"What brings you to Hyde Park this evening?" Catriona attempted a conversation.

"It's a beautiful evening for a walk, but we were just leaving," Lady Henrietta said. "Lord Milington, it's been a pleasure."

"I hope you have a wonderful evening, *Lord Milington,*" Lady Josette said, placing a particular emphasis on the name. Catriona could not miss the undercurrent of unpleasantness, wishing the women would hurry up and leave.

"Until next time, Lord Milington, Miss Beaumont," Lady Rosalie said.

At least one of them had acknowledged her presence. It wasn't much, but perhaps Lady Rosalie Ashmore was only following the lead of her elder sister and her mother. If that was the case, Catriona quietly thought, then she couldn't wait to see how Lady Rosalie acted once she was married and no longer around her parents as much.

Perhaps Lady Rosalie could be a friend.

Catriona was relieved when the Ashmore ladies left and she and Lord Milington were alone again. She noticed that he also appeared grateful they had gone, seeming to relax somewhat. But why?

"Do you know the Ashmores well, Lord Milington?" she asked, looking up at him and finding the complex expression on his face too difficult to make sense of. However, it seemed quite unwarranted by an accidental run-in with the Ashmore ladies.

Was there a history between them? Based on the way Lady Josette had been acting, Catriona hazarded that there might have been something between the two of them. But as far as Catriona knew . . . Lord Milington had been single when she'd first met him.

Lord Milington sighed.

"The Ashmore family has been friends with my parents for many years," he said, sounding reluctant.

He opened his mouth as if he was going to say more, but quickly shut it. That was all the confirmation Catriona needed to know there was more to the story. As she was about to ask what else he had to say on the matter, a flower seller appeared before them.

Lord Milington approached the flower seller without another word. He purchased a bouquet of flowers and presented them to Catriona, and she couldn't help but smile as her heart skipped a few beats.

"They're so pretty. Thank you, Lord Milington." She looked up at him.

"It's my way of apologizing for the unpleasantness that the Ashmores can bring whenever one meets them unexpectedly," he said once they had started back towards the carriage. "They may be family friends . . . but they are a family who can require some mental preparation before meeting them. It was not my intention to bump into them this evening, and I believe you could see how they treated us differently."

"It is not your fault if they chose to behave badly," Catriona said. "If I must choose, I think I prefer being ignored by them than being on the receiving end of whatever feelings Lady Josette harbors for you."

He smiled sadly but said nothing.

Eventually, they arrived back at the carriage, where Lord Milington told her stories of living in the Far East at her request. Anthony had let something slip about his time there, and she was intensely curious. She said it sounded like something she might enjoy reading about in a book, and that his experiences called for their own book to be written, which made him laugh.

"I originally went to oversee some of my father's business interests there," Lord Milington said, "but I found the freedom I had there so great that I decided to stay a few years instead of only a few months. I am glad I stayed so long. If I had returned earlier, I might have entirely missed the chance to meet you as a single man and have the chance to court you."

Catriona blushed deeply at that, which he fond utterly adorable. They arrived at Beaumore Manor once more, and as he helped Catriona down from of the carriage, he pressed a kiss to one of her gloved hands.

"I look forward to seeing you at the Wesington soirée tomorrow evening," he said. "Until then, Miss Beaumont."

"Until then, Lord Milington."

She waved and smiled as the carriage rolled away, then turned to walk up the steps to the front door, with Alice following.

"Well, that was a rather interesting outing," Alice said. "What do you suppose the Ashmore family has against you to act like that?"

"I don't think I care enough to want to know, Alice," Catriona said. "Lord Milington is not worried about it. I don't think I have a reason to be, either."

## Chapter Twenty-Six

As the carriage pulled away from Beaumore Manor, Hamish glanced out of the window to see Miss Beaumont waving at him. He waved back, then watched Catriona and Miss Brown talking and laughing as they walked up the steps to the manor. He smiled. It was wonderful to see them so close.

Hamish sat back against the carriage seat, reviewing their walk in the park. He couldn't help but wonder about his decision to avoid telling Miss Beaumont the truth behind the Ashmores' strange behavior. It may have been easier at the time to avoid it and distract her with the flowers from the flower seller, but he knew she was far from stupid. She was going to grow curious enough about it to ask him sooner or later.

She deserved to know . . .

But did it really matter in the end?

Hamish knew he was already moving away from his father's control and influence. He'd made that decision when he moved to the Far East, though he hadn't told that to Miss Beaumont. It had simply been one of the best decisions he had made up to this point in his life. He knew that courting Miss Beaumont would be another decision that his father might disagree with, but he would live to regret not at least giving the relationship a chance if he were to immediately marry Lady Josette Ashmore instead.

It was indeed Miss Beaumont's behavior that had drawn him to her. She didn't act as though she was owed anything simply because Anthony happened to be friends with Hamish. Miss Beaumont had been genuinely surprised to hear that he wanted to court her properly yesterday. And she had held her tongue and not asked the Ashmores about their odd behavior towards her or Lady Josette's apparent obsession with him.

He hadn't failed to catch the way Lady Josette had been staring at him. He knew Miss Beaumont had seen it, but she had said nothing. He'd done the same. Lady Josette, on the other hand, had only properly addressed him and ignored Catriona completely. If she hadn't been with Lady Rosalie and the Countess of Ashington, he had a feeling Lady Josette might have made quite a scene.

She might have accused Miss Beaumont of stealing him from her, as if they were in a proper relationship. Her father would not like the scandal such a scene would cause, but it would have pushed Hamish to do what they wanted had she played her cards right. Perhaps that was why Lady Rosalie and the countess had been with Lady Josette tonight.

Either way, he decided it was not something he needed to tell Miss Beaumont. Not yet.

The carriage arrived at his estate. Upon stepping into the hallway, he was met by his butler.

"A letter has arrived from your father, your lordship," the man said while presenting him a letter.

"Thank you."

Hamish took the letter and sat down in the small parlor, his stomach knotting up as he looked at the letter. It must have been hand-delivered.

The contents of the letter were not entirely shocking. The duke insisted that Hamish had defied him in the worst way possible by starting a courtship with Miss Beaumont. It ended with his father saying that he would give Hamish one final chance to do the 'right' thing. His father maintained that the right thing, in this case, was to call off the courtship with 'the orphan girl,' as he called Miss Beaumont throughout the entire letter, and marry Lady Josette Ashmore.

*After all, Hamish, this is the most prudent business decision to be made here. The orphan girl has nothing to add to our business. Even if she did, I doubt she would know how to handle it properly. She grew up with nothing, and she is nothing to us. Her party may have been enough to convince the rest of the* ton, *but I refuse to be associated with her through marriage.*

*End the courtship. Marry Josette. That's the right thing to do.*

It didn't even end with a proper signature. Hamish crumpled the letter up.

Without thinking any more about it, he tossed it into the nearby hearth and watched as the flames devoured the hateful letter. His father and the Ashmore family may not approve of Miss Beaumont, but Hamish certainly did.

He *refused* to be like them.

He poured himself a large drink, and somehow, he ended up asleep on the sofa, right there in the parlor.

The next morning, after making sure he did not smell of alcohol and had been properly cleaned up, he called on Miss Beaumont before attending to some more business with Anthony. Having finalized their business indentures, it was time to start getting things moving and make a profit.

He was very excited about the new venture, for it was working with Anthony that would allow him to be independent and oppose his father openly.

"It's a lovely morning, Lord Milington," Miss Beaumont said as they sat in the drawing room. "Why don't we take a walk in the rose gardens?"

"That sounds absolutely lovely, Miss Beaumont," he said as he held his arm out for her.

Miss Brown accompanied them to the rose garden, of course, but that was fine with Hamish. He would rather have a chaperone and be the perfect gentleman for Miss Beaumont than have any whiff of scandal. That wouldn't be easy, not with the Ashmore family and his father so angry that he was refusing to marry Lady Josette. But in Miss Beaumont's company, none of that mattered.

Their walk was largely silent, with Miss Beaumont simply taking in the sights of the garden and Hamish enjoying her quiet company. That was something else he quite enjoyed about Miss Beaumont. They didn't necessarily have to talk to enjoy each other's company. Enjoying a walk together, quietly and happily, was more than enough for them.

However, on the walk, Hamish felt the strongest urge to tell Miss Beaumont what his father had been requesting of him. If he knew the Ashmores and his father as well as he thought, they were going to try and find a way to create some sort of scandal to harm her, or at least threaten to. Then, Hamish might be forced to marry Lady Josette to protect Miss Beaumont. He didn't want to put her through that!

"Lord Milington?"

"Yes, Miss Beaumont?"

"I do believe this is the happiest I've ever been," Miss Beaumont told him. "I'm out of the orphanage . . . and I have found a relationship that brings me much happiness. You, Anthony, the entire Beaumont family, really . . . you've all given me something I could have only dreamt about in the orphanage. Thank you."

"I do not know that I am the one you must thank," Hamish said kindly. "I was only here to help you transition out of that life as an orphan and into life in High Society. It was Anthony who gave me permission to ask you to court me. I think it is Anthony and the rest of your family whom you ought to be properly thanking."

All thoughts of telling Miss Beaumont that his father didn't agree with their courtship fled his mind at that moment. If this was indeed the happiest she had ever been, he would be nothing short of a monster to ruin it for her by warning her of his father's intentions.

They made their way back to the manor, as it was about time for him to meet with Anthony about the business. In the hall, he smiled at Miss Beaumont and kissed her hand.

"I look forward to seeing you tonight at the Wesington soirée," he said. "Until then, Miss Beaumont."

"Until then."

With that, he excused himself and quickly went up to Anthony's office.

As Hamish sat down opposite Anthony's desk, he let out a long sigh.

"How does your father feel about you courting Catriona?" Anthony seemed more concerned with that than with business.

Considering the letter Hamish had received from his father the night before, he couldn't entirely blame his friend for wanting to know where the duke stood on the whole situation.

"He doesn't like it," Hamish said. "I received a letter last night. My father refuses to call her anything but 'the orphan girl,' which I find quite insulting, and he insists that I make things 'right' as he calls it. That means me calling off the courtship with Miss Beaumont and marrying Lady Josette . . . which he and the Ashmores would like to see happen. I'm sure you've seen the way Lady Josette looks at me."

"Like a dog after a rabbit," Anthony said. "She gave you such a look at Catriona's presentation, I thought you would fry. And I assume she did it to try and make Catriona uncomfortable too."

"Or perhaps me for daring to escort anyone *except* her into dinner," Hamish mused.

"Have you *told* Catriona that your father doesn't approve of this courtship?" Anthony asked with a frown. "It's one thing for her to assume Lady Josette is simply jealous that you have decided to court someone else. But it's another thing entirely to know that she's jealous because you're acting on your own plans when she's expecting you to go along with your father's. What if your father decides to find a way to make a scandal out of your courtship to Catriona?"

"I haven't told her anything about it yet," Hamish said. "Besides, she's been through a lot recently. The last thing I want is for her to be upset, Anthony. In the rose gardens, just before I came to see you, she told me that this was the happiest she's ever been. I would hate to ruin that . . ."

"Even if your father plans to ruin it for you?" Anthony raised an eyebrow.

Hamish saw the skeptical look.

"Hamish, nothing good can come from keeping secrets—especially not when we both know your father does not approve of this particular courtship and is still pushing for you to marry Lady Josette."

"I'd rather go to war before I marry Lady Josette, Anthony!"

Hamish almost threw his hands in the air. How could anyone believe there was anything more to his refusal to marry Lady Josette than not liking her personality?

"Be that as it may, Hamish, I don't think this is a good thing to hide from Catriona," Anthony said. "Especially as you are supposed to be properly courting her now. That means that you, on some level, trust her to be part of your life. All of it, *up to and including* the way your father treats you."

"Anthony . . . I'm going to tell her. I just . . . haven't decided on when yet. Besides, there is the Wesington soirée tonight. I'd rather she be able to enjoy that without worrying about what our courtship means for me with the way my father is."

"But your father could take the opportunity to ruin her reputation at tonight's soirée," Anthony warned. "We both know how much he wants you to marry Lady Josette . . . and we both know what lengths he can go to to get what he wants. Remember when you told him you were going to the Far East?"

Hamish nodded.

There was no need to relive *that* scene.

# Chapter Twenty-Seven

Alice helped Catriona into her ball gown for the Wesington soirée. It was a dress of white spider-gauze delicately embroidered with silver acorns, with the flowers Hamish had given her worn as a corsage. Catriona couldn't help but smile as she looked at the flowers.

"You and the marquis are quite the perfect couple," Alice said as they continued to get Catriona ready for the soirée. "You've found your very own Prince Charming, it seems."

"Yes, I have," Catriona said. "Alice, I can't help but enjoy the time I spend around him. Is it odd that I want nothing more than to have a good night with him? He was so polite and the picture of gentlemanly grace when we went on our walk around the rose gardens."

"I can see why you are so fond of the time you spend with him," Alice said. "He has such a beautiful manner."

Catriona nodded.

With the dress properly laced up and Catriona's hair done up in curls, Alice put the final adornment for the night in place. It was a small tiara that, Bridget had told her, had once belonged to Catriona's mother, presented to her upon her marriage. It was not the most fashionable tiara, but it was . . . special.

It was, perhaps, the only thing of her mother's that still remained in the manor.

"Oh, if only your parents could see you," Alice said. "I have no doubt they would find you the picture of wealth and grace in this outfit."

"You think so?" Catriona turned to look at her friend, who only nodded firmly at her.

"Now, I do believe you're ready for the carriage. Come on, then," Alice continued. "You have a prince to dance with tonight, and I think everyone else is waiting for you."

Catriona nodded. Already, they had taken far too long. They went downstairs and out to the carriage.

Bridget and Anthony were indeed already waiting for them, but they had only just arrived themselves, it seemed. They looked exquisite in their outfits, and Catriona felt her stomach sink a little. Bridget and Anthony had been raised in this world. What if Catriona could not perform as expected at this soirée?

While she had done well at her presentation ball, she worried that without everyone helping her through the evening, any of the ladies might start gossiping if she did anything the least unladylike.

"Ah, there you are, Catriona," Bridget said with a smile before Anthony helped her into the carriage.

"Catriona, what a lovely outfit . . . oh, your mother's tiara . . " Anthony almost couldn't stop staring. "It looks exquisite with your dress. Did Bridget get it for you?"

Catriona nodded.

"Well, it will be the first time it's seen a ball in many years," Anthony said. "I believe your mother was only able to wear it once before . . . well, before she passed away. I wish your father had been able to raise you properly. But he'd be quite proud of you now. I know it."

Catriona mouthed her thanks to Anthony as he helped her into the carriage. To hear that from Anthony meant a lot.

Once Alice and Anthony had gotten into the carriage, a footman pulled the door shut for them. Then, it was off to the Wesington manor for the party.

The carriage ride started quietly, as the nervous tension meant they were all far too anxious to speak. Until Bridget cleared her throat.

"We have some wonderful news to share with you," Bridget said.

Anthony's face paled a little, but the smile on his lips and the sparkle in his eyes told Catriona another story. Was it good news? Or bad news? Catriona couldn't fathom his curious expression, but she nodded for them to continue.

"I'm with child!" Bridget cried triumphantly. "We're going to tell the rest of the family at dinner tomorrow evening, but . . . I couldn't wait to tell you."

"So that's it!" Catriona said, squeezing Bridget's hand. "Oh, that's wonderful! Congratulations."

"Thank you, Catriona," Anthony said. "It's an event we've been waiting for, and it's finally here."

Though she was happy for Bridget and Anthony, she couldn't help but think of having children of her own . . . with Lord Milington. It would require a marriage, of course, but it would be something so wonderful she could hardly wait for it. It felt almost cruel that they were required to court first, but she knew there was a good reason for it.

It was what was expected of them. Though Catriona wished it didn't matter, she knew there was no way around it as the daughter of the late Viscount Beaumore.

The carriage arrived at Wesington Manor just moments later, bringing Catriona's private thoughts to an end for the time being.

It didn't take long for Anthony to help all the ladies out of the carriage. A butler met them at the front door and escorted them into the ballroom. Catriona almost missed seeing the Dowager Countess of Wesington standing waiting for her guests as she admired the beautiful decorations in the ballroom.

"Ah, Miss Beaumont! What a pleasure it is to see you could come," the dowager said. "It is an honor to have the *daughter* of the late Viscount Beaumore here at my soirée."

"Thank you for inviting me, my lady," Catriona responded with a polite curtsey. "This is a beautiful ballroom."

The Dowager Countess of Wesington thanked Catriona with a smile, then excused herself to go and greet some guests who had come in behind them. Catriona, meanwhile, couldn't stop staring at the beautifully decorated ballroom in front of her.

She was just taking in the lovely fresh flowers, the green and white banners, silver streamers, and the three large chandeliers overhead blazing with light when she saw Lord Milington walk into the room. His blue long-tailed coat was perfect with his the white waistcoat and black knee-breeches. Catriona thought him outstandingly handsome, and she glowed with pride to think they were courting. He was the model of an English gentleman. And he was hers.

Her heart began to thud as she took in his appearance and the way he seemed to almost float towards her through the crowd.

He bowed when he drew level with her, and she dipped a small curtsey in return, beaming at him.

"It's lovely to see you this evening, Miss Beaumont," Lord Milington said, gazing into her eyes and making her shiver with pleasure.

"And you, Lord Milington," Catriona replied, blushing.

She was suddenly quite glad that Alice was there too and could act as chaperone if need be. Alice was there to keep her reputation from being tarnished, and Catriona knew she must do everything she could to avoid risking her good name. Sometimes, she forgot how to think straight when she was with Lord Milington. Catriona didn't know what might happen if she were to go alone with Lord Milington into the gardens, but it made her catch her breath.

"I'm glad you've arrived safely," Lord Milington continued. "And in such a beautiful gown tonight, as well."

Catriona had no chance to reply before she noticed the Ashmore family had arrived too . . . and they were walking right towards herself and Lord Milington. The Earl of Ashington looked rather sullen, his eyes half-hooded, and his mouth turned down. The women, on the other hand, all looked rather smug, Catriona thought. Each one had a polite smile painted on, but they were all false. She knew how to spot a fake smile from her time at the orphanage, and it was clear to her that something about the situation didn't sit right with the Ashmore family.

"Lord Milington," the Earl of Ashington started, "it is a pleasure to see you. Would you please send my regards to your father? I wish him a speedy recovery."

Without any of them acknowledging Catriona, the Earl of Ashington simply walked away, accompanied by his ladies, sniggering behind their fans. Catriona wondered what kind of people could be so rude and thoughtless as to giggle over the illness of one of their father's good friends.

"Is everything all right, Lord Milington?" She pursed her lips and frowned slightly as she looked up at him, unsure what to make of the encounter.

"Yes, there's nothing to worry about, Miss Beaumont. I want you to enjoy the evening," Lord Milington said.

Catriona could hear the uncertainty in his reassuring tone. He seemed under strain, as if he was holding back something more than just concern about his father's illness.

In that moment, she realized that his reluctance to say anything directly about his father had not been limited to this interaction with the Ashmore family. No, it was indeed universal. He refused to speak about his parents with her, which automatically had her wondering why.

Could it be that Lord Milington was hiding something about the duke and duchess, and he just didn't know how to tell her what it was? Or was it simply that there had not yet been an opportune time to tell her, since they were always chaperoned?

He must have some good reason for not discussing his parents with her. She resolved not to go looking for a reason, even though it stung a little to think he might consider her not worth telling. Nevertheless, it was troubling . . .

Her thoughts were interrupted by the orchestra striking up the chord of the evening's first dance set.

Lord Milington turned to her with a smile.

"May I have this dance, Miss Beaumont?" He offered her an arm.

"Of course, you may, Lord Milington," she said, taking it.

They pushed their way to the dance floor. On the way, Catriona decided there was really no reason for her to worry about why he had not told her about his parents. Either he was worried she would not be accepted by them—which was a fair point to consider, since she had been raised in an orphanage, which appeared to prejudice some people against her—or he was worried she would feel unwelcome in some other way.

As he took her into the proper dancing position, Catriona took in a deep breath. Dancing with Lord Milington would help her let those thoughts go, let them no longer influence how she behaved that evening. She didn't want to make things any worse for him, after all.

If they were going to have a proper courtship, she needed to trust that he was always going to be a perfect gentleman. Perhaps there was a legal reason why he was staying quiet, something that might be affected by knowledge of their courtship.

The orchestra started playing, and Lord Milington started to guide her around the dance floor. As they twirled around, as before, Catriona pretended they were the only two on the dance floor. The tip had helped so much at her own ball, and she so wanted to make a good impression on the Dowager Countess of Wesington this evening.

*Mine was probably a last-minute invitation . . . and I want to make the* ton *proud!*

# Chapter Twenty-Eight

Hamish felt terribly guilty that he hadn't yet been completely honest with Miss Beaumont about his father. There was no real reason for him to hide so much from her. His Grace did not approve of the courtship, but Hamish had decided before asking Anthony to court Catriona that he did not care what his father approved of. Especially not since his approval came at the cost of marrying Lady Josette. That was something Hamish could not bring himself to do.

As he danced with Miss Beaumont, he could not stop thinking about the Earl of Ashington's greeting and his mention of the duke's illness. Surely, Hamish thought, if Father was really gravely ill, Mother would have sent word to me. There would be no reason for her to hide it . . .

He decided that, for now, this wasn't the best way to spend his time. His focus must be on Miss Beaumont, and it was going to be a beautiful evening with her by his side, officially. With him as her partner, she seemed to have no problems on the dance floor.

The dance set couldn't last long enough for Hamish, for he so enjoyed the feelings dancing with Catriona gave him. But the music eventually faded, and he had to escort Catriona back to the side of the ballroom. He wanted to dance another set with her immediately, but Hamish saw the Dowager Countess of Wesington approaching them.

He steeled himself to be scolded for something, but the dowager was all smiles.

"Lord Milington, I hope you do not mind if I steal Miss Beaumont for a while," the countess said.

"I do, my lady, but how can I refuse?" Hamish joked.

He then reached for Miss Beaumont's hand.

"Save the last dance for me, please, Miss Beaumont."

"Of course, Lord Milington," she said with a smile.

Hamish couldn't help but smile back as the dowager countess took Miss Beaumont away, and he chuckled softly as he heard the older woman say, "Would you like a tour of my home, Miss Beaumont? It's most renowned for . . ." Nevertheless, he felt the loss of his partner.

He had just started towards the refreshment tables when he spotted all three Ashington women—Lady Henrietta, Lady Josette, and Lady Rosalie together—walking towards him. The last thing he wanted was to have to dance with Lady Josette out of politeness because they happened to be standing near one another when the next set began.

He rapidly decided that refreshments could wait until he was sure the Ashmore family had found some other man to bother for a while.

He instead escaped into the garden through a door that happened to be open nearby. Sending a quiet prayer up to heaven, he started to walk around the gardens. It was a beautiful spring night, and he was sure that, eventually, others would come outside too.

However, he knew there was no reason for him to worry about that for the moment, so long as he didn't come across any women unchaperoned.

As Hamish wandered around the gardens, he resolved not to keep the truth from Miss Beaumont any longer. As he came to his resolution, he realized he had stumbled upon the orangery. As beautiful as it was, he didn't want to wait there for Miss Beaumont. She deserved to enjoy her time with the Dowager Countess of Wesington first.

He would tell her the truth about the duke the following day. She deserved to know that the duke hated the idea of him courting 'the orphan girl,' and that he'd rather see Hamish marry Lady Josette. It would also be a good time to reassure Miss Beaumont that, no matter what happened, he was willing to defend her against any nasty rumors His Grace might decide to spread because Hamish preferred her to Lady Josette.

He was even willing to walk away from a mighty allowance for her.

That should have been all she needed to know about his character. And he felt stupid for not telling her the day before, or even in the rose gardens at Beaumore Manor earlier that day. Having seen how insistently the Ashmore family was trying to talk to him, and having heard the Earl of Ashington very deliberately give him the news that his father was *supposedly* gravely ill only made him wish he had told her earlier.

It might have explained why the three Ashmore women looked so incredibly smug when Lord Isaac had shared the news about his father's illness.

His thoughts were interrupted by footsteps. He hoped it was Miss Beaumont and the Dowager Countess of Wesington, though there was no reason to suppose they would come out there to look for him. Hamish hadn't even gone inside the orangery proper. Instead, he stood by the doorway, leaning against the building.

He turned to see who had come out to join him, only to have his stomach twist upon locking eyes with Lady Josette. His blood froze, knowing she was there with him—entirely without a chaperone! Anthony had warned him earlier to be careful. This was indeed the perfect chance for the Ashmore family to try something to force his hand into marrying Lady Josette.

And he had been stupid enough to walk right into their trap.

"Hello, Hamish," Lady Josette said with a large smile. "I'm so glad to have a moment away from the stuffy ballroom."

"You ought not be out here without a chaperone, Lady Josette," Hamish said, not moving from his spot. This had to be played very delicately.

If someone else walked in and saw them together, the situation could be misconstrued, and they would both be compromised. He would be deemed to be acting inappropriately, being alone with a lady. And people were much more likely to believe Lady Josette over him . . . especially since he was now courting Miss Beaumont officially. He would be forced into marrying Lady Josette.

But Lady Josette only laughed at him, as if she were flaunting her power over him.

Hamish's stomach sank to his shoes. He wanted to run away, but there was nowhere to run to. She had blocked the exit leading back to the ballroom.

"Are you so concerned for my reputation, Hamish?"

The fact that she addressed him so intimately, as if to make a point, confirmed his suspicions. He had to get away from her, and he had to do so without allowing anyone a chance to misconstrue the situation.

The sooner he could tell Miss Beaumont of this, the better. But he knew it hardly mattered what he did or said—Lady Josette would tell the scandal sheets that he had taken her out into the gardens alone at the soirée, and thus, the damage would be done. And it would be done entirely with her parents' approval, as well as his father's.

"I ought to return to the ballroom."

With that, Hamish started to move to pass Lady Josette, but she moved to block his path again, this time moving so he would have to physically touch her and move her out of his way to pass her. She fluttered her lashes again, clearly intent on her task of ensnaring him, uncaring for her reputation.

A shiver ran down his spine. The encounter was no accident. She had engineered things *intentionally* . . . to force his hand into marrying her. His anger rose. How despicable the whole family was to stoop to such low tactics to make sure their will prevailed.

It only further confirmed for Hamish how much he did *not* want to marry into the unscrupulous tribe.

"I really . . . I must go."

He had no chance to make another move to leave before a high-pitched gasp filled the air. A lady's high-pitched gasp.

Hamish looked up from Lady Josette to find the Dowager Countess of Wesington, Miss Beaumont, Lady Bridget, Lady Rosalie, and Lady Henrietta staring at him.

"Let go of my daughter, Lord Milington! *How dare you!*" Lady Henrietta broke the shocked silence that had fallen after the gasp.

Lord Isaac appeared on the other side of the path, and Hamish's cheeks flushed as light dawned on him. This was a full set up by the Ashmore family. Every single one of them must have been in on it, and they had made sure that the Dowager Countess of Wesington, Lady Bridget, *and* Miss Beaumont would witness it too.

"If you know what is good for you, Lord Milington," Lord Isaac said coldly, "You'll do the *honorable* thing."

The implication made his stomach sink further.

Hamish looked to Miss Beaumont as a commotion erupted, leaving him no chance to defend himself. But what was there to say? The look on her face left him feeling as though Lord Isaac Ashmore had personally kicked him in the gut.

Her eyes wide, jaw slack, and tears brimming in her eyes, Miss Beaumont could say not a word to him. He could not accurately describe her expression, but there was no doubt that the Ashmore's had achieved their double aim of hurting her and ensnaring him. His heart squeezed as he looked into her eyes pleadingly, to no avail.

Without another word, both Miss Beaumont and Lady Beaumore turned and walked away from the scene. Lady Bridget wrapped an arm around Miss Beaumont's shoulders as they disappeared from sight.

Hamish wordlessly, helplessly, watched. He was surrounded by Ashmores. There wasn't even a way for him to chase after Miss Beaumont, to explain things, though he desperately wanted to. The Ashmores would not allow him to comfort the woman he was courting . . . and that hurt him as much as it had now hurt Miss Beaumont.

The Dowager Countess of Wesington took in the drama, and then hurried away—most likely to repair whatever damage she could before the scandal erupted. Hamish's reputation would be indelibly stained if he did not do the right thing . . .

One by one, the Ashmores left, but Lady Rosalie remained with Lady Josette.

"You should have listened to your father, Hamish," Lady Josette said. "Our marriage *will* happen . . . and your hand is forced now. Forget the orphan girl. She's nothing. Our marriage? That will be the biggest party held this Season. I'll make sure of it."

Her tone was sweet, but the words dripped with the jealousy he had seen etched on her face every time they had met when he was escorting Miss Beaumont.

"Just because you have forced my hand into this marriage does not mean that I shall ever be happy in it, Lady Josette," Hamish finally said. "Do none of you realized that the reason I have not pursued this marriage is because I wish to be happy? Not everything rests on a business deal."

He shook his head and started to move away from the ladies. They didn't stop him.

At least, until it appeared that he intended to go after Miss Beaumont, when Lady Josette grabbed his arm.

"Leave the orphan girl alone. That's an order."

"You're not my mother, Lady Josette," Hamish said as he pulled his arm away from her. "And I must at least try to fix the mess you've caused. I would not be a gentleman if I did not try. That is why you want me, no? Because I am a gentleman?"

Lady Josette looked as though he had slapped her across the face, but he didn't care.

By the time he arrived back at the ballroom, however, Miss Beaumont had disappeared. All the Beaumont family had gone. It wasn't a good sign. He went outside to see if their carriage was still there, but he only managed to glimpse it from behind as the carriage pulled away from the house.

No!

# Chapter Twenty-Nine

Catriona's eyes remained puffy the next morning. She'd cried herself to sleep after Alice had hurriedly taken off the gown from the ball. Finding Lord Milington in the garden with Lady Josette last night had been terrible. Her heart had broken in that moment, and she now believed she would never feel whole again.

How could Lord Milington meet Lady Josette like that in the garden? And after having seemed so sincere in his wish to court her. Had he set her up so she would seem nothing more than a woman of no consequence to High Society? Or was he truly *not* a gentleman and simply didn't care about her reputation in the way he had claimed to when the original scandal sheet calling Catriona 'plain' went public?

She didn't bother to get out of bed. She simply pulled the covers up to her shoulders and stared at the ceiling, contemplating what in the world had come over Lord Milington. But all she could think about was how hurt and offended she felt.

*How dare he do such a thing?!*

It explained why he had seemed so unnerved at the ball, she thought, her mind in a whirl. She thought she knew why too: He'd wanted to break off their courtship off—and he couldn't simply do it to her face in private. He had wanted to do it in the *most* dramatic way possible, so that everyone witnessed her humiliation.

Because who from the *ton* would want to marry a woman who was raised as an orphan?

The door to her bedchamber opened, interrupting her thoughts. Catriona leaned up and looked over, seeing Alice and Bridget entering. She laid back down, not wanting to hear what they had to say but not wanting to make a scene either. She had done that last night . . . and she didn't want to repeat it.

"The family will be arriving in the next hour, Catriona," Bridget said softly.

"I don't wish to see any visitors," Catriona replied as she turned away from them. "Can I not have a day to myself?"

"I'm afraid you'll have to attend the family meeting," Bridget continued. "We have to do as much as possible to protect your reputation. You've only just been presented to the *ton*. This is the worst thing to happen in that situation,. We need to discuss what happened if you want to be able to continue in your new life."

Catriona sat up with a sigh, propped on her elbows.

"What does Lord Milington's betrayal have to do with my reputation, Bridget?" Her voice quivered as she spoke.

"You were courting him," Bridget said. "That connection alone will be the cause of much gossip. Believe me, it's better if we get ahead of it now rather than let the gossip come to us and handle it as it comes. The last thing we want is for you to be dragged into any unnecessary scandal, Catriona. That's really what this meeting is meant for: to keep you from harm."

She supposed Bridget had a point. There was a lot that could have gone even more awry than things had last night, even though they had left the soirée as soon as they realized what had happened with Lord Milington. It simply didn't make sense to her that the *entire* family now wanted to talk about it. But, then again, judging by the doubt with which some members of the family had regarded Lord Milington's presence at the manor from the first, she told herself she should not be surprised that everyone was coming.

Catriona nodded slowly, pushed herself off her elbows, and got up. Alice helped her into a morning dress, but Catriona felt numb and felt no enthusiasm when she saw how pretty it was in the mirror. There was no cheerful conversation that morning.

When she was ready and she and Bridget headed for the drawing room, Catriona could felt the lump return to her throat and a pit in her stomach open up. Lord Milington had been the perfect picture of a gentleman . . . before the soirée. Now, she wasn't sure what to think of him.

When she entered the drawing room, she saw the rest of the family were already there. Catriona noticed how strained Anthony looked, and they hadn't even started the discussion yet! Then again, Lord Milington was his friend. She supposed the events of last night were weighing on him as much as they were on her. Anthony had been the one to give Lord Milington permission to court her, and now it seemed he had made a grave misjudgment of the man's character.

"I never liked Lord Milington! Not from the start of this entire escapade of getting Catriona presented properly to the *ton*," Lady Spencer started. "How can we be sure he wasn't the one to spread the original rumor saying Catriona had not yet been presented because she is too plain? Is there any reason to believe he ever had her best interests at heart now?"

"Enough, Margaret," Anthony said, an edge to his voice. "The best thing we can do now is not make accusations." He cleared his throat, and then continued, "Our main priority is to focus on Catriona's reputation and well-being."

Catriona didn't like the way he spoke, but she remained silent. If that was their main priority, she was not going to question it. Honestly, she would rather talk to Lord Milington and tell him how much the scene had hurt her, seeing him with Lady Josette like that. But she knew that was only going to make things worse, especially if she did it without a chaperone there herself.

"We will all support you, and I personally will do everything in my power to repair the damage," Anthony finished. "I . . . I feel guilty that this has happened, as it was I who gave Lord Milington permission to court you—"

The way Anthony cut himself off before he could say more intrigued Catriona, but not nearly enough for her to want to know what he was hiding. Anthony could protect Lord Milington's secrets for all she cared. She didn't want to hear them now.

"Thank you, Anthony."

Catriona's voice was quiet, and she felt she had nothing more to say.

"Oh, chin up, Catriona," Eleanor said briskly. "If he is willing to meet a young lady unchaperoned in the gardens while he is courting someone else, then Lady Josette has provided a service to us. We do not need *that* sort of person associated with our family."

"She's right, Catriona," Margaret added. "I believe he has done all of us a favor. But in doing so, he has also done us a great disservice."

"Enough. All of you," Anthony said. "Lord Milington has done something horrible, yes, but we cannot speculate on his actions now that he has done the deed. All we can do is make sure that Catriona is not adversely affected by them."

"If you'll all excuse me," Catriona finally said. "I trust you all enough to let you discuss how to go forward. I'd like to return to my bedchamber now."

The family nodded in awkward silence.

Alice followed her up to her bedchamber. Catriona sat on the window seat, looking out across the gardens of her manor. She may not have had any wish to go outside, but the calming effects of contemplating the gardens could not be overstated. She'd always felt happy and at home among nature . . .

But now all she wanted was to return to the orphanage. There, no one knew anything of the importance of a lady's reputation. She would have avoided all this if she had only remained at the orphanage. If Mr. Dilworth had left her alone . . . But then, she wouldn't have been able to live in such a beautiful manor, with a family who loved her. She would still be stuck serving and cleaning in the kitchen, wearing nothing but a dreary gray dress.

Alice sat with her, reading a book in the corner. Neither of them had anything much to say until one of the other servants brought lunch into the room.

It was then Catriona realized she had not even eaten breakfast. She had not been hungry that morning, but her stomach growled a bit at her now. Still, she felt no wish to actually eat.

However, knowing that no one would like to see her faint, she decided to try.

She'd fainted once in front of the family. She didn't want to repeat that.

As she nibbled on some of the assorted fruits that had been brought up to the bedchamber, Alice looked over at her.

"Catriona . . . I'm so sorry this has happened," Alice said, her eyes sympathetic. "But I'm sure there's a good explanation for what you say happened last night between Lord Milington and Lady Josette."

Catriona heaved a heavy sigh as she put her fruit down.

"Even if there is an explanation . . . it's too late."

Catriona couldn't stop herself from bursting into tears at the thought of Lord Milington marrying Lady Josette.

He was supposed to be *her* Prince Charming, wasn't he? So why had he gone off and done such a stupid thing such as getting caught with Lady Josette when she was unchaperoned, and he was courting Catriona?

She buried her face in her hands as she let the tears run. It wasn't but a moment later that the food was moved from beside her and comforting arms wrapped around her shoulders.

"Oh, Catriona . . ."

Alice attempted her best to comfort Catriona, but there was no comfort in the world that could take away the hurt she felt in that moment. It helped to have a shoulder to cry on, though. There was nothing to alleviate the pain, but at least Alice *tried*.

"I thought I had found a man who did not care that I grew up an orphan . . ." she sobbed.

"I know, Catriona. I know," Alice said quietly. "What Lord Milington has done is horrid, but Lady Josette is also just as culpable, and we both know she was jealous of the way Lord Milington had been paying attention to you before you were officially courting him."

Catriona didn't say a word, but the thought struck her. Alice was right. She remembered something about the reason why the Ashmores were feared in High Society because of their liking of starting rumors about people they didn't like. Lord Milington, Anthony, and Bridget had all thought it was the Ashmores who had spread the rumor in the scandal sheets that she had not been presented to the *ton* because she was extremely plain.

"I don't care what Lady Josette thinks," Catriona managed to say. "You do not go after a man who is courting someone else. Not in that manner. You wait until the courtship ends, if it comes to that."

"Well, I don't think Lady Josette and Lord Milington are accustomed to waiting," Alice told her.

Alice held her close as Catriona tried to calm down. Nothing really worked to calm the hurt or shift the lump in her throat, but Alice didn't try to stop her from crying. Instead, her friend only wiped her tears when they fell down her cheeks and let her sob as much and as hard as she needed to in order to feel better.

Catriona didn't care what Lord Milington had been trying to do when he had been caught with Lady Josette the night before. All she cared about now was making sure she couldn't be hurt in that way ever again. For now, that probably meant courting anyone was no longer an option. The men of High Society were too . . . judgmental, though that conviction could just be an aftereffect of having had her heart utterly shattered.

"Why don't we go for a walk around the manor?" Alice suggested, clearly attempting to get Catriona to do something other than wallow in her sorrows in her bedchamber. "It's a beautiful day. Perhaps seeing some of the beautiful scenery will distract you, even if only temporarily?"

"Thank you for trying, Alice, but I have no desire to go anywhere today," Catriona said. "Please . . I just want to take a day to mourn the loss of what I thought was going to be a good relationship. A proper courtship . . . as you said yourself . . . to a proper gentleman."

Alice nodded slowly.

"I'll see what kinds of puddings the kitchen has left over, then. Sweets and a good book ought to do you some good," Alice replied.

Catriona nodded and let her go quietly.

# Chapter Thirty

Two days after the disastrous soirée at Wesington Manor, Hamish lay in a daze on his sofa. The night before had been utterly horrid too, as his father had called in on him. Strangely, the duke appeared to be the picture of good health despite Lord Ashington's claim otherwise. He'd had the cruel audacity to call in to congratulate Hamish on his forthcoming betrothal to Lady Josette Ashmore.

What didn't seem to matter to His Grace was that Hamish had only offered his hand in marriage to Lady Josette because it was the honorable thing to do. As much as he hated to admit it, Lord Isaac had been—he knew Hamish was too much of a gentleman not to do the honorable thing in the circumstances.

Having overindulged in spirits to drown his sorrows after his father had left, Hamish had no urge to get off the sofa and lie down in his bedchamber. His days of being a bachelor would be over by morning, he thought darkly. Somehow, Lord Isaac had found a way to get them a special marriage license to allow them to marry almost immediately—after Hamish had been forced to propose to Lady Josette.

The whole thing reeked of a set-up, but the reactions of the guests at the ball had not reflected that at all despite the Ashmores' unscrupulous reputation.

"Lord Milington!"

The butler's deep voice startled Hamish, as he had been lying on the sofa with his eyes closed.

"Your mother wishes to speak to you. It's urgent, she says."

"Show her in," Hamish said as he sat up.

Moving proved to be a bad idea. The moment he moved, it felt like a boulder had begun to roll around his head. Overindulging in drink now seemed to be almost as horrid an idea as it had been to be caught alone with an unchaperoned Lady Josette.

It took a few moments, but his mother was soon seated beside him on the sofa.

"Good morning, Mother," Hamish said, his head cradled in his hands.

"I would ask what has happened, but I am well aware of what might have caused your condition this morning," she said. "Hamish . . . I must confess something to you. Your father was absolutely furious when you refused to go through with a marriage to Lady Josette Ashmore."

"He threatened to cut my allowance off if I continued to court Miss Beaumont," Hamish informed her. "I am well aware he was not keen on the arrangement. What does this have to do with what happened at the ball, Mother?"

"Your father and Lord Isaac colluded to have you caught in a compromising situation with Lady Josette," his mother revealed. "They knew you would be far too honorable to do anything *but* offer her your hand in marriage if you were caught with her without a chaperone. When you stole off into the gardens at the Wesington soirée, they saw their chance. I attempted to stop Lady Josette from going out, but Lady Henrietta found a way to keep me from going after her daughter. I do not know if she was in on the plot . . . but the entire Ashmore family is patting themselves on the back for stealing you away from Miss Beaumont. I refuse to use the same phrase as your father to describe her."

Hamish nodded softly. It may not have been much, but he appreciated his mother standing firm with him in his refusal to speak ill of Miss Beaumont.

"Why are you telling me this, Mother?" He turned to her. "The deed is done. I am to marry Lady Josette tomorrow morning by special license. Father has won, unfortunately."

"No, no he has not. You do not wed until *tomorrow*." His mother looked him firmly in the face. "The last thing I want to see is you suffer the same fate as me, dear boy. I know you cannot be as ignorant of how unhappy the marriage is between myself and your father as you sometimes appear to be. It is a lonely existence to have dreamed of marrying for love and found yourself trapped in a marriage without any at all."

His mother now looked down at her hands.

"You may not have your father's temper, but I fear Lady Josette as your wife will take all the joy out of your life. Look at how you have spent the last couple of days. Do you wish to feel this way for the rest of your days? If so, then go ahead and marry Lady Josette Ashmore." She looked up at him now, her eyes pleading. "Go to Miss Beaumont if you would rather live as you see fit. Make things right. You still have time. It will not be easy . . . but nothing worth doing is ever easy, Hamish."

He took his mother's hands in his and squeezed them softly.

"Thank you, Mother," he said. "For telling me that, and for confirming my suspicions. I was not sure it was a set up when everyone's reactions at the soirée felt so . . . genuine. Miss Beaumont deserves a proper explanation, and I was contemplating how best to tell her that Father does not approve of us courting when Lady Josette appeared..."

"Then go." His mother stood up. "Go. Make things right."

He nodded.

His mother excused herself from the room. Hamish cleaned himself up and did his best to nurse his hangover. But he decided there was something important he must do first before trying to make things right with Miss Beaumont.

His father must learn that he would not stand for this kind of manipulation any longer. He would not be controlled, and there was nothing his father could do to make him marry Lady Josette. His own good reputation was already going down the drain, so his actions no longer mattered.

Besides, Lady Josette deserved whatever harm came to her reputation because of her part in the cruel charade. She had been the one to do the meddling on their parents' bidding.

The carriage ride to Mildenwoode Manor felt far too short that day. It was now or never, and if he was going to marry the woman he was utterly sure he loved, then he was not going to waste any more time feeling sorry for himself. The only way to find a way to be with Miss Beaumont would be to tell the duke outright to leave him alone.

When he arrived, he went straight to the drawing room, finding His Grace standing in front of the hearth with a glass of brandy in his hand. *Probably drinking to congratulate himself on my marriage to Lady Josette.*

"Your Grace," he said coldly.

"Ah, Hamish," his father said. "Have you come to discuss the details of the wedding?"

"You have no right to meddle in my life this way," Hamish said as calmly as he could manage. "I will not be marrying Lady Josette. You cannot make me."

The duke now turned to him with a sneer on his face.

"I did it for your own good," he said. "And another word on this matter, and I will be sure your mother pays the price for it. You *will* go through with the marriage."

"Just because you have made your own marriage unhappy does not mean you can force me to do the same," Hamish ground out. "And, by the way, Mother is coming to live with me, and if you hurt her in *any* way, so help me, I will kill you."

He gave His Grace no chance to respond, turning on his heels and leaving the room.

As he walked out of the manor, his hands shook. As he got into his carriage to leave, all he could think of was protecting his mother . . . and making sure that Miss Beaumont knew what a horrid mistake he had made.

The same wealth of courage he'd felt when telling his father that he was leaving for the Far East hit him again now, buoying him up.

"Take me home," Hamish ordered the coachman.

The journey home took too long for his liking, but at least it gave him time to think things over. Once again, he resolved that his father was not going to be allowed to stop his son from following what he felt was the right path.

When they got home, Hamish alighted from the carriage and told the coachman, "Do not go anywhere. I shall not be long, and we have one more stop to make."

He went inside, to find his mother standing in the entry hall, with the butler attempting to calm her down.

"Mother, it is all right," he said as he walked in. "You need not worry about him. His temper shall trouble you no longer. You shall stay here with me."

He pulled her into a tight embrace.

"I thought you were . . ."

"I wanted to be sure you were safe first." Hamish looked down at her. "I could not bear to think that he would hurt you to make me do as he wishes."

He now looked to the butler.

"Have my mother's lady's maid and a couple of footman go to Mildenwoode Manor. Bring back everything Lady Milington needs. She is to have any chambers of her choosing here."

"Of course, my lord."

He looked at his mother as he pulled away from her.

"Now, if you'll excuse me, I have one other person to talk to." He managed a smile. "I must go to Beaumore Manor. Immediately."

"Take care, Hamish. And good luck."

He kissed her cheek in farewell and went out to the carriage.

When he arrived at Beaumore Manor, despite his nerves, he could hardly open the carriage door fast enough.

He leaped up the steps to the front doors and knocked.

"I am here to see Miss Beaumont," Hamish said when a maid opened the door.

"I am sorry, my lord, but her ladyship is not seeing anyone just now."

Hamish's heart sank. The maid went to close the door, but Anthony's voice stopped him.

"Hamish . . . you . . . have you slept at all in the last two days?" Anthony asked, coming into view behind the maid.

"That's not what matters, Anthony. Where is Miss Beaumont? I've made a grave mistake, and I must make sure she hears the explanation from me alone," he pleaded.

Anthony nodded tiredly. "She is in the ballroom. Come in." Anthony dismissed the maid as Hamish stepped inside. "I don't know what happened at the soirée, Hamish, but if you make this any worse for her . . ." he added warningly.

"I know, Anthony."

With that, Anthony led him to the door of the ballroom and left him there. From outside the door, which stood ajar, he could hear Miss Beaumont and Miss Brown talking. He surmised that, whatever they were doing in there, it was probably an attempt to distract her from the utter disaster that their courtship had become at the soirée.

He poked his head around the door. The two women were sitting talking, and when Miss Beaumont saw him, she gasped, and both sprang to their feet.

"Lord Milington! What are you doing here? I am not receiving visitors today," she exclaimed, frowning at him. "Please, leave at once

"Miss Beaumont . . . please," Hamish said. "I know you have no desire to see me, but I must insist you hear me out."

"Oh, and what could you possibly have to say to me?" Her voice quivered. "You are to marry Lady Josette tomorrow. Is that not what you wanted all along?"

"No. Quite the opposite, in fact. You have been misled by my father's actions" Hamish began, but she cut him off. He saw her glance at Miss Brown, who nodded almost imperceptibly and moved back further into the room, he supposed to give them some semblance of privacy. But she kept her eyes on him.

"What could your father *possibly* have to do with this?" Miss Beaumont snapped. "Could you not see how she looked at me when we danced at my presentation? And when you escorted me to dinner that night? She has always wanted you to pay attention to her in the same way—"

"The way I pay attention to you, yes," he said. "I am well aware of it. Her father feeds that wish of hers, calculating that a marriage between his daughter and me presents him with a lucrative business opportunity too good to miss out on. As does my father."

"I see," she said, head held high. "And what kind of financial benefits did you expect to get from Anthony by marrying me?"

The way she narrowed her eyes, the coldness of her voice, cut him to his core. She was accusing him of paying attention to her for the same financial reasons as the duke in wanting him to marry Lady Josette—like some common fortune hunter!

"None," Hamish replied, swallowing his pride.

Being honest was his only option, he knew. It should have been his policy right from the start, he realized now.

"Oh, I can as easily believe that as I can that you love me."

Miss Beaumont cried, turning away from him, her shoulders shaking. If only she knew how much he wanted to comfort her.

"Please, leave me, Lord Milington. I have no desire to hear your explanations. They are as pathetic as they are unnecessary."

"You'll forgive me for believing otherwise, Miss Beaumont," Hamish pressed on, determined to tell her all whether she liked it or not. "Miss Beaumont, my father has . . . certain peculiarities when it comes to how I live my life. Has Anthony ever told you the main reason I went to the Far East?"

"I said *leave me*, Lord Milington," she said more strongly. "Alice, please call for the butler, will you?" Miss Brown nodded and started towards the door. Hamish realized he had almost run out of time. She had to hear it now.

"My father never approved of our courtship, and he and the Earl of Ashington designed that encounter between Lady Josette and I to force me into the marriage they have had planned for me since before I left for the Far East," Hamish told her in a rush. "I left to escape his controlling manner, and it gave me something I never thought I could have—a wish to live my life in a way that makes me happy."

Miss Brown stopped at the door, but that was only the second most interesting thing to happen. Miss Beaumont turned to face him.

"I'm sorry. I think I must have misheard you. You said . . . they what?"

"That encounter in the gardens at the soirée . . . While you were on your tour with our hostess, I decided to leave the ballroom and go for a walk in the gardens. I wanted some time alone to think how best to tell you that my father did not want me to court you," Hamish went on, desperate to get it all out before she banished him forever. "I was about to return to find you, to invite you on a walk the next day, when Lady Josette approached me. Unchaperoned. She engaged me, Miss Beaumont."

"And yet this has not appeared in the scandal sheets. Why not? If it is true, do you not think that other gentlemen deserve to know what kind of women come of the Ashford name?" Miss Beaumont took a couple steps closer to him, and his body grew hot. "You could save someone else the heartache of it all."

"I must admit that I have been . . . too overcome by the shock to do much until today." He rubbed the back of his neck. "But, Miss Beaumont, it was never my intention to hurt you. You may ask Anthony or even Lady Josette herself. I doubt even Lady Josette will hide it if she thinks her reputation is safe from tarnish."

"Why ought I to believe Anthony?" Miss Beaumont started towards the door. "Where is the butler, Alice?"

"He knows I would never behave in such a way. If he thought so for a minute, he would leave me to hang by the scandal sheets, and he would have every right to do so in protecting his family name. But I *cannot* abide my father forcing my hand into a marriage I never wanted." He turned to face her as she continued towards the door. "I chose to court you, Miss Beaumont, because you had no designs of gaining my heart solely to better your life financially."

"Then why court me at all? It seems all the *ton* is worried about is reputation and bettering their own lives," she said, her voice almost cracking now.

"You were not afraid to be yourself in my company." He walked closer to her. "You told me of your life in the orphanage openly, even though I could have rejected you for it."

She moved away, refusing to look at him.

"Miss Beaumont, what can I do to show you that I never wanted to hurt you?" Hamish was at the end of his rope, and he knew it was only a matter of time before Miss Brown opened the door and actually called for the butler.

"Leave me alone, Lord Milington. You have done quite enough damage to my reputation."

With this, Miss Beaumont opened the door and rang the bell for the butler herself.

"Miss Beaumont, I fell in love with you," Hamish said, his voice catching on the words. "Nothing would make me happier than to wed you, and I must take the blame for involving you in all this . . . mess. I shall leave you now, if that is what you wish, but please . . . one word from you, Miss Beaumont, and the wedding with Lady Josette shall not happen tomorrow morning. I ask you to think, at least, on that offer. Will you marry the poor man who made the mistake of not being honest with you from the beginning, but who adores you and will always love you?"

He turned towards the door, not expecting an answer. But her voice stopped him in her tracks, and he turned back.

"If that is so, then why did you entertain the lady in the gardens, Lord Milington? Why entertain the desires of a woman you say you cannot stand to marry?"

"I had no thoughts of her at all, only of you. The whole scheme was a plan by my father and the Ashmore's to trap me in a compromising position—Lady Josette made sure she had no chaperone when she cornered me by the orangery. When I pointed that out to her she laughed. I panicked because I knew the implications if we were caught together. I tried to move past her, but she intentionally blocked my path multiple times, making it necessary to lay hands on her to get by. Of course, I couldn't do that . . . then, lo and behold, the rest of the Ashmores arrived, plus the other important *witnesses, including yourself,* needed to verify my misbehavior." He paused, while she looked at him attentively, her face still stained by tears. His heart went out to her, but he knew it would be disastrous to try to touch her.

"I can only imagine she was so jealous of us courting, she carried out the plan to the letter, to destroy your reputation and mine, and have the satisfaction of forcing me to marry her. She must have realized that the main reason I did not wish to marry her was because I had fallen in love with someone else," Hamish told her. "And if you take nothing else from this conversation, please know that I shall be absolutely miserable being married to her . . . though I believe I deserve it to a degree for hiding the truth from you."

"So," she said, looking at him. "One word from me and the wedding is off?"

"Yes. One word from you, and I shall call the wedding off. My reputation will suffer because of it, but I imagine that will repair itself once all is known to a wider audience."

Hamish, now prepared to do almost anything to win her back, moved towards her dropped to one knee, gazing up at her imploringly.

"Forgive me for this, but . . . will you marry me, Miss Beaumont?"

She did not move, and he felt as if his heart would burst of she didn't answer soon.

She took a deep breath, meeting his eyes.

"I-I . . . *yes*, Lord Milington, I will," she said firmly, reaching out to take his hand and pull him up.

"You will?!" Hamish stood up, wondering if he had heard correctly. "You'll marry me?"

"I should be honored to be your wife," she said, and he folded her in his arms, weak with relief.

"Thank God for that," he sighed, his nose buried in her sweet-smelling hair.

# Epilogue

Anthony had stepped up to walk Catriona down the aisle. Since her parents had both passed away, her father just months before all of this had begun, it meant the world to her that Anthony was glad to fulfill that role.

"Are you ready, Catriona?" He looked at her, his arm extended. "Hamish awaits us."

Catriona could not hold back a smile as she took his arm. This day had been months in the planning, and she could not have been any happier with the way things had happened.

After Hamish had proposed to her, he had called off the wedding to Lady Josette. His father had indeed cut off his allowance, and his mother had moved in with Hamish permanently.

But in the end, all that mattered was that Catriona was to marry him.

As Anthony walked her down the aisle, she felt as if butterflies filled her whole body upon seeing Hamish standing beside the vicar at the end of the aisle. He looked so extremely handsome in his wedding suit she almost swooned to think he was hers!

She also felt quite happy they had decided not to have a grand wedding for all the *ton* to see. It was an intimate ceremony, only close friends and family allowed. So, the Ashmore family had not been invited despite their close ties to Hamish's family. Catriona was happy at their absence.

They reached the end of the aisle, and Anthony handed her off to Hamish.

Hamish looked at her with a handsome smile on his face. There could be no denying that they had fallen irrevocably in love with each other, Catriona believed.

"I, Hamish, take you, Catriona, to be my wife," Hamish said. "For better or worse, for the rest of my life. I could not survive the journey of life without you at my side now that we have met. With you by my side, I will be the happiest man on earth."

Catriona felt her cheeks heating up. The vicar then turned to her for her vows.

"Hamish, I have fallen ever so deeply in love with you," she started, her voice growing stronger. "I know you have come to know me well, and that you respect my wishes. To have this wedding today is all the proof I need to know that you'll keep me loved and warm for the rest of my days. *Knowing* that you are to be my husband for the rest of my life is more than enough for me to know just how deeply, how truly, you love me . . . and I hope that I can show you how much I love you throughout the rest of our days together."

"I pronounce you man and wife," the vicar said at last, with a wide smile. "Lord Milington, you may kiss the bride."

Catriona and Hamish shared a sweet kiss before pulling away, to the cheers of the family and friends who had been invited to watch their special moment. He held his hand out to her. She took it, and they went with the vicar to sign the register in the vestry, where Catriona took great pleasure in signing her new name.

After the ceremony, everyone returned to Beaumore Manor for a wedding breakfast. Bridget had done her best to arrange it for them, and Catriona was grateful to her family for all they had done to help her and Hamish celebrate their day.

She would not have had it any other way, especially not since she had Hamish at her side. In fact, the other reason she would not have had it any other way was because Alice could attend her wedding as a friend instead of as her lady's maid. Lady Spencer had offered her own lady's maid as a stand-in for the day, which both Catriona and Alice very much appreciated. The day would not have felt so right if Alice was not there in church to see Catriona wed.

"I propose a toast," Anthony said as everyone gathered for the wedding breakfast, "to the happy couple. For having overcome many trials already, and for the strength they have shown the rest of us in that time. To Catriona and Hamish!"

"To Catriona and Hamish!"

The rest of the wedding party cheered for them. Catriona's smile widened. She raised her glass in toast with the rest of the guests in attendance, then to her husband. He toasted her back and they shared a glance. Fortunately, once the food was served, things quietened down enough to allow for quiet conversation as they ate.

Hamish leaned over to his wife. The smile on his face told her that he was just as happy to spend the day like this as she was, but she had a feeling that he was excited for more than one reason.

"And what brings such a lovely smile to your face this morning, my wife?" Hamish whispered to her.

She loved the way he called her 'his wife,' and honestly, that alone was more than enough to make the day worth the wait.

"I have everything I have always wished for now," she replied. "A loving family . . . and a dashing Prince Charming for a husband. It truly has worked out for the best."

He nodded slowly as his smile widened.

"And it'll only continue to be a good life now you are a proper part of the *ton*," he replied. "You have the money and the freedom to do so much more than you could have ever dreamed possible at the orphanage. What do you want to do?"

"For now? I want to enjoy our wedding day. We can spend the rest of our lives having fun and doing what we can to better London. But today is all about us. Let us keep it that way, Hamish."

He nodded.

# Extended Epilogue

Three years after the wedding, Catriona and Hamish could hardly say that their life had not been blessed. As Catriona watched her young son play with his wooden horse, she could hardly believe this was her life now. Their son, Jonathon, was a great addition to their lives. Though Catriona bore the marks of carrying the child in her, she was more than proud of the way her life was going.

In fact, the money she had been left by her father had gone a long way towards funding a project that she had always thought London needed—an orphanage which provided orphans with a good education *and* a loving environment. The orphanage in which she and Alice had grown up had only provided those things to a point . . . and she had heard horror stories of other orphanages from the people who came to adopt from Mrs. Easton's orphanage.

"Jonathon! Come on," Catriona said. "It's time to go inside."

As much as she loved the garden, it was indeed time to take her son inside. There was nothing more for them to do outside, and there was actually something she had to do. Well, that she and Hamish had to do. They would be leaving Jonathon with his nanny for now.

"There you go, grab the horse, yes," she said as she walked over to him. "Come on then. There we go." She picked him up.

Her son giggled and put his arms around her neck in a hug. She squeezed him softly before carrying him back inside. Though most of the *ton* would have considered her odd for being so involved in her son's life, she knew it was what she wanted. She had not had the kind of parents she'd wanted, and she wanted to be sure her boy got those he deserved.

So far, she had done well to avoid her mother's fate, but for that reason, Jonathon would be the only child she would ever have if she could help it. Another child could risk her and the baby's lives. Hamish understood that, thankfully.

As they walked into the manor, Hamish came along the hallway leading into the gardens.

"There you are, Catriona," he said. "I've been looking everywhere for you. Are you ready to go and check in on our orphanage?"

"Almost, Hamish. Let me get Jonathon up to the nursery," she said. "I'll meet you by the carriage."

He nodded. On her way past him, he stopped her momentarily to peck her cheek before letting her go. Catriona could not help but smile.

How had she been so lucky as to have someone so caring as Hamish as her husband?

The answer didn't really matter to her, for she was deeply content that she had found someone like Hamish. The fact that he had been willing to make things right, even when it seemed all hope was lost, had brought them their current happiness.

Catriona put Jonathon down on the floor in the nursery as Alice walked in behind her. Alice had not wanted to work in the new orphanage, as much as that might have been a good place for her. Instead, she was now Jonathon's nanny, though she still did a lot around the house, too.

"Thank you so much for taking care of him today, Alice," Catriona said. "You remember how to do everything?"

Alice nodded.

"I do, Catriona. It'll be fine," Alice soothed Catriona. "You're not a bad mother for wanting to keep him here while you're doing other things. It's all right to admit that he cannot go everywhere with you."

Catriona took a deep breath.

"Thank you for that, Alice."

With that, Catriona hurried down to the carriage to join Hamish. But when she arrived, she found Hamish waiting outside the vehicle.

"May I hand you into the carriage?" Hamish grinned, extending his hand to her.

She smiled, taking it.

"I would quite like that, yes," she replied playfully.

He helped her into the carriage and got in himself. The door shut behind them, and off they went to the new orphanage.

"How is Miss Brown? I feel as though I do not see her often," Hamish remarked.

"She is well. She's happy looking after Jonathon," Catriona replied. "And how is your mother? You wrote to her, didn't you? How is she?"

"She is faring well too," Hamish replied. "Apparently, my father is still quite bitter that she left him, but she is happier now she is out of the manor. I plan to keep the apartment for her, but she may be better off moving here with us."

"Oh, I think that would be absolutely lovely, Hamish," Catriona said, hearing the hope in his suggestion. "She would see Jonathon every day then, and I think that would be the best way to keep her from your father. We can instruct the servants not to admit him further than the front door."

"What about outside the main gates? Is that far enough, do you think?" Hamish added jokingly, and they both laughed.

Then, he let out a sigh.

"But today is not the day to worry about how my mother and my father are. All I can do is be thankful that it was she who came to me to tell me that my father had a part in attempting to force my hand . . ."

Catriona took his hand in hers.

"And now, you have a beautiful family and an orphanage to take care of," she said. "Your mother deserves the best we can give her, to thank her for helping you realize that there was still time to fix things before you were no longer able to marry me."

Hamish smiled at her, squeezing her hand back.

The carriage rolled to a stop at that moment, as they had arrived at the new orphanage. As they walked in through the entrance, the headmistress came to greet them.

"What a pleasure it is to have you here today, my lord, my lady," she said, curtseying. "A young baby girl was brought to the orphanage a few days ago. I thought you might like to meet her."

"Of course." Catriona smiled.

It was always bittersweet to see another young girl arrive at their orphanage. Hamish put a hand on her shoulder to comfort her as they walked through the orphanage to meet the young girl. The other girls and boys in the orphanage all knew them by their faces, which was a good thing. It meant they knew who to look for if something terrible had happened and they needed help immediately.

Being removed from the day-to-day operations was hard for Catriona, but it was for the best. She would have been far too emotional to make most of the decisions which required good logic. The decisions she did make, though, were to do with what had affected her the most adversely as a child, like what to do with the older children, how to treat the children, and even what kind of schedule they had as a whole throughout the orphanage.

The headmistress smiled as she showed them the baby girl in the crib.

"Oh . . . Hamish . . ." Catriona sighed as she looked down at the baby girl swaddled in her crib fast asleep. "She's so pretty . . . how could someone leave her here like that?"

"She may not have originally been wanted," Hamish said softly, "but that doesn't mean no one will want her."

"*I* want to adopt her, Hamish."

He looked at her, surprised. "Well, we can do that if you wish, Catriona. What shall we name her? I think we ought to at least have a name before we finalize the paperwork."

"Elspeth," Catriona replied. "We can name her after my mother. Elspeth Charlotte Middleton."

"I like that name very much," Hamish said. "It honors both our mothers, the mother who gave her life to bring you into this world, and mine, the one who risked everything to be sure that we could be happy together."

Catriona smiled.

Hamish turned to the headmistress.

"Bring us the adoption paperwork. She shall have a proper childhood with us," he said. "Thank you for showing her to us."

The headmistress nodded, clearly pleased.

Catriona carefully lifted the young baby from her crib. The child stirred in her sleep but did not wake. Instead, she woke and cooed at them. Her tiny body wriggled in the swaddling, and then she got her arms free.

The young child held her arms out to Catriona, who laughed in delight, though her eyes shone with tears as she held the baby close.

"Oh, Elspeth . . . yes, Elspeth fits her so well," Catriona said as she turned to Hamish. "Would you mind filling out the paperwork so that I can hold her? I . . . I don't want to set her down now I've picked her up."

"Of course, Catriona," he said. "Why don't you sit down with her, and then we can fill out the paperwork together? I'll write everything, except your signature, but it will give you a chance to make sure everything is just so."

Catriona nodded.

They found a place for her to sit—in a rocking chair on the other side of the room. She sat down with Elspeth in her arms and looked down at the child, her face alight with joy. The baby was happily clutching Catriona's hand tightly, as if there was good reason not to let go.

The headmistress returned with the paperwork. Catriona, Hamish, and the headmistress all went through it together. It was long, but it was all they needed to do other than pay a fee to take Elspeth home.

Once everything had been taken care of, Catriona carried the young child through the orphanage as they took their tour of the place. Most things were in good condition, though some of the mattresses had worn out a little quicker than she had expected. That was all right. They could do some investigations and find better mattresses to purchase this time, ones which were comfortable but wouldn't wear out as quickly.

While they walked, Catriona's heart filled with love for each of the children who had been left there. She told all the children, once they were old enough to understand, that she too had grown up in an orphanage. She also told them that she had experienced something out of the ordinary and that she was there to make sure they all had a happy life in the orphanage.

She told them that they were each other's family, a special family who grew up together in the orphanage while they waited to find out what life had in store for them. It was one of the ways she had coped, thinking of herself and Alice as sisters, and she quite liked the idea of encouraging the children to think the same way.

Eventually the tour came to an end.

"Why don't we go and surprise my mother?" Hamish looked at her as they were leaving the orphanage. "My mother has always wanted a granddaughter. I think she will fall in love with Elspeth instantly."

"I think so too," Catriona said. "But let us wait until tomorrow. She's fallen asleep . . . and I would hate to wake her up to meet any of the family, other than perhaps Jonathon tonight."

They both looked down towards Elspeth to see she had fallen asleep in her little dress, cuddled against Catriona's chest. Hamish only smiled a little wider at the sight.

"If that is what you wish, then that is what we shall do," he said. "To the manor?"

"To the manor."

The carriage journey back to the manor was quiet, for they both wished to let Elspeth sleep during the ride. Upon their arrival at the manor, Catriona took Elspeth up to the nursery. Jonathon had outgrown his crib, but they had not yet put it away. She quietly thanked providence for that.

Alice and Jonathon were playing in the nursery when she walked in with Elspeth. Alice saw the young girl in her arms first, and quickly told Jonathon to quiet down and go and say hello to his father, who was waiting downstairs for him.

Then, Alice walked over to Catriona.

"What's her name, Catriona?" Alice didn't bother to ask where they had gotten her, or why. She already knew.

"Elspeth Charlotte Middleton," Catriona whispered back as she put the baby in the crib. "She was dropped off at the orphanage a few days ago. When I saw her . . . I knew . . . I just knew I had to adopt her. Is it wrong to believe that I'll be doing that more often now we have a few new cribs set to arrive soon?"

"I think you are doing the world a service by raising the orphans," Alice replied. "You will actually love them, and you're starting slowly, so you can ensure they get the best care possible. Those you cannot personally take care of will still get the benefits of your love through the orphanage you have set up." Alice put a hand on Catriona's shoulder. "You're the kind of person we wanted to see walk through the orphanage doors when we were younger, and I'm so proud that you have become that woman."

Catriona smiled.

"I am too."

They walked out of the nursery to find Hamish coming towards them with a now half-asleep Jonathon in his arms. Catriona gave her son a big hug and a kiss goodnight before they put him down to sleep too, telling him that he needed to be quiet for his little sister.

Jonathon ended up falling asleep on the mattress to his bed, which they helped him to move, as he insisted on being next to Elspeth for the night.

He barely knew her, and yet, he already cared so much for her.

Finally, Hamish and Catriona walked to their bedchamber side by side, his arm around her shoulders, smiling broadly.

"Jonathon certainly takes after his mother," he told her. "The way he wanted to sleep near Elspeth tonight . . . I can see you wanting to do the same if you were still a young child. You've taught him well, and I think that says a lot about you, dear wife." He pecked her on the cheek affectionately.

"You think so?" Catriona grinned, raising her brows.

"I do. You have raised Jonathon so far to be a loving big brother, and he has only now gotten a little sister. I think you'll be a wonderful mother to *all* of our children, no matter how they come into our family." He pressed a soft kiss to her cheek. "You're going to be amazing at anything you do, with all your love behind it. I've seen it time and again, and I was lucky enough to be one of the first recipients of your love."

"Thank you, Hamish."

They walked into the bedchamber. Catriona was thoroughly exhausted from the excitement of the day, but she was quite content to know that she now had her own family. A family that would keep on growing, keep on bringing them both joy and happiness.

Made in the USA
Columbia, SC
04 December 2024